MW00615577

Other tales in the series:

Playscript:

LISEL'S SHAWL

Merilyn Wakefield

1995

Cover design and photo by Merilyn Wakefield

Acknowledgement to Sunni Bates for her assistance

Printed by aBCD Printing Company, Seattle, Washington

mwynhad

ISBN 0-9657993-2-8

With appreciation for Malissa White who shares the vision for this world.

LISEL'S SHAWL

Cold winds swept down off the Mountain that winter leaving layers of frost on walls, roads, fences, and all else that dared stand outside. Inside the castle cold eyes frosted with disbelief at news of the death of the Mountain King.

Tiberius brought the news. Old news, he admitted, and not improved by age, but he had been out of the castle since Grand Parade, and just that morning heard it himself. "The Mountain King is dead."

Lisel, the King and the Chief Steward, sitting together as they did many winter days, did not immediately rush upon him with questions they must eventually ask. They stared as if more willing to believe Tiberius had not arrived in their midst than to believe he brought such news.

"An accident--apparently his horse slipped on the way up the Mountain and went over a cliff," Tiberius continued, relentless with the unpleasant news.

"A terrible road," the Chief Steward muttered recalling the terror of his one trip up the Mountain.

"And how do we have this news?" asked the King.

"One of my officers saw it," Tiberius replied. "Horse and man, over the edge, to an abyss so far below he could scarcely see where they landed."

"And how did your officer see such a thing on the Mountain?" Lisel inquired. Her face turned pale and her hands folded into hard white knuckles.

"I sent him to follow. The Mountain King traveled alone and drank, an accident might..."

"When?" Lisel cut him off. "When did your man follow him?"

"As he went home, after the wedding," Tiberius said and with due respect to men who drink too much, uncorked his jug.

"Months ago!" cried the King. "Why do we hear so late?"

"I just heard myself," Tiberius repeated. "I sent Jurgius to keep an eye on him while I went on Grand Parade and since then I've been in the Western Provinces. Only last night when I returned and heard the report..."

"The death of the Mountain King is not a matter to wait for a routine report!" The King rose to pace the room. "We are speaking of my Wife's father!"

"A ticklish situation," agreed the Chief Steward.

Ticklish? Ticklish is the best you can do? Lisel thought.

"Jurgius thought it best to hold his report for me rather than trust runners with such news," Tiberius said. "The man is dead; quicker report won't undo it."

"And gossip makes a bigger mess," agreed the Chief Steward.

"What do you mean, gossip?" snapped Tiberius.

The Chief Steward drew back from the hot

breath. "Only that it's a bit...a bit...embarrassing that he should have a fatal accident on the way home from his daughter's wedding."

Now the Chief Steward paced opposite the King. The two of them swirling about the room could make a man dizzy, but Tiberius drew again on the jug and waited.

"Embarrassing?" Lisel could contain herself no longer. "All you can say about the death of a king is, embarrassing?"

"It IS embarrassing," said the King, "and covering it up doesn't make it look any better."

"Nothing has been covered up," Tiberius said with patience as if he explained a matter resolved so long ago that it no longer surprised him. "He reported, I reported..."

"Rather long in arrival, that report," snapped the King.

"Perhaps," Tiberius agreed, "but done, and you wouldn't have wanted your Wife to receive such news on Grand Parade."

The King grimaced.

"Never a good time for bad news," the Chief Steward tried to placate them. "Today we have it. Today we make the best of it. Perhaps best not to dwell upon exactly when the accident occurred--just announce that it happened."

"Anyone, even my Wife, will ask how we came by the news," the King fretted. "Looks bad, very bad."

"Why did you send a man after him?" Lisel asked.

"Seemed unsafe," Tiberius said. "I told Jurgius to give him his distance but keep an eye on him."

"Not much use sending him if he couldn't help. Maybe no one could help on that road, and he did drink so..." The Chief Steward sighed in resignation.

"The Mountain King did not drink more than any of you and held it better," Lisel declared. She did not believe this accident or that Tiberius heard of it the first time last night. She felt outraged how banally they discussed the matter.

"I only brought the news. I didn't do it."

"Has anyone accused you?" snapped Lisel.

"You, by your eyes," Tiberius returned.

"The bearer of bad news is never welcome, but no one can accuse you; you were on Grand Parade," The Chief Steward intervened.

"I'm glad to have witnesses for that!"

The King still paced. "This looks exceedingly bad for us. My Wife must be told, and an announcement of some sort..."

"Mourning," the Chief Steward said. "What about that?"

"Mourning will only advertise it and cause discussion, but if we don't--that looks bad too." The King paced back again.

"If you hadn't sent your man following him we wouldn't have this embarrassing problem, would we?" Lisel drew her shawl tightly about her shoulders and left the room.

"At least not until Spring..." the Chief Steward was saying as the door closed behind her.

The draft when she shut the door caused the King to halt mid pace and go after her, but he found the passageway empty.

Spring--Lisel had longed for spring, anticipating her visit to the Mountain King.

"You will tell me what passes here and I will tell you all that passes on the Mountain," the Mountain King had said. She had been saving news to share with him: anecdotes to warm his smile, hard questions to discuss, tapping each other's wisdom. Now the ultimate news, *they lie about your death*.

She heard the King call down the passageway after her, but did not answer. Let him call. She must sort this out before saying another word. Already Tiberius read in her eyes how she did not believe him, how she accused him.

The mantle of responsibility fell onto her shoulders with a crushing weight--too soon. She had expected to have time to learn from the Mountain King, time to spend on the Mountain, time to ease herself from the affairs of this court. Now in one blow the weight of the Mountain fell upon her.

Lisel did not light her lamp or rake up the fire in the hearth in her dark chamber. She did not invite the commiseration of the Chief Steward, though she heard him pass and pause outside her door. The cold dark suited her mood for sorting hard thoughts.

Did she believe the Mountain King was dead? The mountains looked no different tonight than last night when she thought of him snug in his mountain home, before a roaring fire, dozing with a hand to Rufus' head, dreaming of her. Did she believe he had been dead last night, and the night before that and almost every night since she last saw him? No--too cruel to rip back all those nights of imagined communion, counting time until Spring. Easier to believe he died this cold winter day in the blast of Tiberius' report.

She did believe the Mountain King was dead; no advantage to Tiberius to make up such a story. That he had been dead a very long time without her knowledge she could not yet face. That threw her into a whirling darkness as wild as if she too went over the cliff. That notion she would have to get used to over time; develop skill at walking the cliff edge without vertigo. All she could face for one night, the first night, was--dead. She did not know how clearly she faced even that one fact. She slept sitting in the chair, wrapped in blankets, and did not dream.

Dawn did not offer Lisel the reprieve of momentary forgetfulness. She woke knowing exactly why she had not gone to bed, why her neck ached, why her limbs felt stiff, why her heart pumped cold at the center of her body.

"This is what it means to be a queen." She

recalled how the Mountain King once touched the tears on her cheek. No kind finger marked them this morning. This is what he meant by, "step apart as an equal to become a Ruling Queen in the privacy of your own counsel."

Lisel splashed her face with cold water and examined her eyes in the glass above her basin. Today she must keep counsel with herself and find whatever wisdom she might draw from the memory of the Mountain King. To do so, she sought fresh air outside the walls of this castle, polluted by lies. She pulled on boots and layers of skirts and wraps. A warm shawl wound around her head and a hat she tied over that. Nothing but her eyes showed as she stepped out into the biting cold morning. An excellent cold morning, she decided, as she walked downstairs, across the courtyard and out the gate; an excellent stinging cold to blame for the tears in her eyes.

Walking, she felt stronger and the exertion warmed her core under the clothes and socks and boots and wraps. Her breath puffed gray, matching the sky and mists that rolled about the hills outside the castle wall. She knew before she passed through the gates where she headed; out the road toward the Northeast Province where the sheep belonging to the castle an old sheepherder kept flock. She wanted to touch something of the Mountain today and chose the sheep, her own woolly lamb and those given in the dowry by the Mountain King. The road, long and hard enough to require exertion, stopped her mind from slamming itself against the truth. She concentrated on the destination that promised simple pleasure, and put aside her grief for the moment.

The thin line of rising smoke, another shade of gray against the gray sky, marked the place Lisel turned off the road and crossed the field toward the shack kept by Danny, the sheepherder. His dogs spotted her and trotted out to inspect her boots. By the time she could see his door, she could make out the image of Danny himself, winding a muffler and following his dogs out to meet her. He waved an arm slowly back and forth. She waved back, reflecting his measured signal.

"A good cold morning to blow you all the way here," Danny said, stamping his boots and smiling on unexpected, though welcome, company.

"A cold morning all right," she replied. She could not bring herself to the falseness of saying a good morning, nor immediately share her grief. To look in the smiling face of one who did not know the awful news made it not true for the moment. "I came to see my lamb--how her winter fleece grows."

Danny grinned. "Thought that's what you might be after. Come along; she's down over this way."

"And the others from the Mountain?"

"Not many left." Danny tramped ahead with his breath circling out like pipe smoke.

"What's become of them?" She ran a step to catch up. "Not lost?" She could not bear more loss today.

"No, not lost; the Chief Steward said to divide them between the Provinces, which I did, except for a few I kept."

Lisel had to half run to match Danny's stride. The dogs circled and trotted around them, as if people like sheep should be kept tight together when on the move. Lisel almost forgot her cares. She recalled skipping by her long legged father; out to see to sheep in a field not far from here, in another time, in what seemed another life.

"There," said Danny, pausing to rest a foot on the low stone wall that marked one field from the next. "There she be, off by herself, and the others--see? Over there--they don't mix."

Lisel climbed over the wall, not easy in all those clothes. Danny had to catch her arm and unsnag her skirt from a thorn bush. She whistled, the way she had called when she kept her lamb in the castle confines.

Nothing looks as silly as a sheep trying to remember something, then catching on and come trotting in too much wool, as if too many skirts. The ewe tumbled straight onto Lisel, tipping her down hard on the frosty grass. Lisel laughed and hugged her, like a child.

"Look at her!"

"Big enough?"

Lisel felt the rich fleece--such wool! The silly sheep pushed her face into Lisel's face and baa-ed her grassy breath, remembering other things.

"A treat," Lisel laughed. "Oh yes, I have one in

my pocket, if you let me up, old girl."

Danny pulled the ewe back with one arm and offered the other to help Lisel rise. "Look at her ears, long floppy things. We never had sheep with funny ears like that, not even the other mountain sheep have ears like hers."

Lisel like the flop-eared sheep; a softer, sweeter look, she decided, than tight, small-eared sheep.

"Fine sheep the Mountain King brought, every one a fine animal," Danny said. "Never seen nothing like them."

"A fine man, the Mountain King," Lisel said. She filled her lungs with the searing cold air.

"True," said Danny. "He came out here a few times, to see about the sheep, how they were getting on with me. Surprised me, a king taking a hand with sheep, but he sure knows his animals."

Lisel clenched against the ache in her chest.

"He sorted me out on a thing or two about sheep," Danny said.

"Sorted me out on a thing or two about myself," Lisel said.

Danny chose to look toward the snowy mountains rather than at Lisel. He likely knew the rumors about the affection between her and the Mountain King. "S'pose we'll see him again?"

Lisel shook her head. "No, we won't. He's dead."

Danny sat down on the wall as hard as if butted by the flop-eared sheep that still pressed close against them. "Dead? No! Old maybe, but not close to dying, not that man."

"An accident." She spit out the ugly words--a nasty, most unnecessary, accident that left the world without the Mountain King moving quietly among his people, sorting them out on a thing or two.

Lisel appreciated Danny's stillness, his quiet sadness and shared respect for the Mountain King.

"Did you want to see the others?" he asked after awhile. "I can send a dog down to bring them up."

"Let's walk," Lisel said, but they did not walk far before Danny noticed, "you're done in, Lisel. Let's stop for a hot drink."

Lisel agreed to Danny's suggestion and they changed course toward his shack. Now she had seen her lamb and let loose some inner pressure by announcing the Mountain King's death, she did feel undone. They sat on crates at the side of the shack, watching the silver sun ball force its way through the overcast sky. Lisel wrapped her gloved fingers around a rough mug of Danny's hot broth and felt warm again.

"I'm okay now," she said after awhile. "I feel so awful, I can't even walk, then it passes."

Danny nodded. "Accident, had to be an accident. Death certainly never meant to be happening to such a fine man."

She couldn't tell him about the road and Blazer. That made it sound like Blazer's fault and neither she nor Danny would find fault with that fine horse. To say more would raise the issue of an accident by

11

man's hand. Patient Danny did not ask questions.

"Will you need help with lambing this year, Danny?"

"Always need help with lambing," Danny replied watching the mountains like he too had trouble imagining them empty of the Mountain King. "Hard work, lambing."

"Do you think I've forgotten?"

"No, you come on down, if the mood suits you. Way the weather's been shaping we'll see lambing before shearing this year."

They never did walk down to see the half dozen sheep left from the dowry flock. Winter days were short and Lisel knew she should start back.

"I'll see them next time," she decided. "Might be soon as tomorrow, or as long as next week."

"Anytime," said Danny, "but next time eat before you start such a long walk. Don't be letting yourself faint with hunger."

He filled her with hot stew before she left. Then she knew she'd be back soon to replenish him. His sisters, living further into the province, didn't provision him so far ahead he could afford hungry guests. Yet she accepted his food and ate well, feeling it less tainted than anything the castle offered.

Anticipation of her goal had warmed her journey to the sheepherder's shack. On the way home she felt the hot stew in the center of her body but the afternoon shadows were colder and the destination less desirable. She had been out all day, taken some pleasure and comfort, but made no advance in her thoughts. Her limbs, her mind, the world itself moved with nightmare slowness.

Outside the castle walls, safely out of view, she stopped to hug a bare oak tree so big she could scarcely put her arms around it. She pressed her face and body into the rough trunk and longed for the hard chest of the Mountain King. The bark scraped her cheek and the pain diverted her attention from the ache in her heart.

The Mountain King was dead by foul play and all they had been able to consider was how to avoid embarrassment and minimize their guilt. By that they had acknowledged guilt, whether they confessed it or not. To think she once vacillated, even one moment, over leaving this place! To think she ever felt the tiniest compunction at turning her back on them! She should have married the Mountain King and ridden away with him on Blazer to the Mountain. She would have been with him to either go over that abyss together, or stand and fight beside him.

Regret, the bitterest part of grief, surged through Lisel and tore at her until she wretched and spilled Danny's hot stew onto the cold ground. Then she leaned against the tree and cried. At last her work began, the crying, the breaking loose down under the layers of tight bindings.

"Takes a year to get through a grief," Lisel often counseled others. She'd counted a year of grief for each of her children and now another grief year rose up to strike when she felt less resilient. Lisel felt old that winter afternoon leaning on the oak tree; old enough to know she would never love again, same as she knew after her last baby that she would never have another child.

What had she to show for a life of hard work and trying to do right? Precious little. Anger, lovely warm boiling anger, restored her energy to walk again toward the castle. Winter evening light turned the snowy mountains purple behind the black silhouette of the castle. The lighted windows did not draw her.

"If you know in your heart you mean no threat..." the Mountain King once said of her conflicted loyalty to a Court that she had served so long she did not know how to untie the knot.

"I mean them no threat," Lisel answered now, "but no longer will I concern myself with this Court. They have not reciprocated my care."

Her pace increased. She stepped to a quicker beat. In the privacy of her own counsel that winter evening she understood how a queen cannot have divided loyalty. She felt no conflict of loyalty now and no regret over her choice.

When the King wanted to see his Wife in private he visited her. He never called her to his chamber because her disturbing presence seemed to sully the peace of his retreat. However, when the King wanted to see Lisel, he called for her to come to him because

14

he liked the fragrance of her presence.

He decided to put off telling his Wife about the death of her father until he talked to Lisel. However, she removed herself from their company for a full day; a very long day for the King, in which he faced, as squarely as he faced any unpleasant fact, that Lisel still loved the Mountain King. Out of sight did not mean out of mind to her. He saw her return through the castle gates after dark. The great relief surging through his limbs gauged how much he had worried about her. The King desperately needed her but decided not to call for her. He wanted to do something for her, and the best he could imagine was going to her, rather than calling for her.

He knew where she kept her chamber but never visited there; always, he called her to him. On that night, in the chill outer passageway, he felt a moment of hesitation before knocking at her door.

Lisel opened the door with her cheeks still rosy from her cold winter walk. Her genuine surprise to see him at her door, he misconstrued for pleasure as she drew him inside.

"What is the matter? Are you alright?"

"I wanted to see you, but not put you out, asking you to come to me," he began, as tongue tied as a new suitor.

"My goodness!" She looked even more surprised. "I do appreciate that. I've been on a long walk and just now got my fire up."

He looked around her chamber feeling like he

had stepped out of now into the past. Lisel's room looked the way he remembered her provincial cottage; bundles of herbs hung from the beams to dry, and shelves were lined with neat rows of medicinal crocks. A covered loom stood to the side of the room. Baskets, shawls, and other simple tools of her daily life crowded comfortably together in her chamber.

"Sit down," she invited.

Strange, he generally gave directions and invitations, but he took the chair where she gestured.

The boots she had worn that day dried by the fire, curled with damp, and tongues hanging out like tired dogs.

"So charming," he observed. "So like your cottage on the farm. Do you remember?"

"I suppose," Lisel said, hanging her wool socks before the fire, "I live the same as always."

"So strange," he murmured, "to sit together before a cottage fire, like nothing between then and now happened."

"Plenty happened." Lisel refused to let him slip into nostalgia. "Let me pour you a hot drink."

"I did not come for you to wait on me," he protested.

She poured hot wine and pressed it into his hands, then one for herself. Across the hearth, on her own terms, she leaned on the mantel and studied him, as an equal, as any man. She found it sad, how handsome he looked with his thick brown hair and short clipped beard. His lean arms with soft hair, disappeared into a fine wool tunic--one she made herself.

What a waste of a fine looking man, for I do not love him, and he does not love his Wife, passed through her mind. "What brought you?" she asked.

"I wanted to do something for you," he said, "and now that I'm here, I haven't the slightest idea what to offer."

Lisel sat opposite and took out her knitting. She preferred to keep her hands busy and this might take him awhile. She knit a few stitches, then realized the work on her needles was a tunic for the Mountain King. She had selected her biggest needles, and heaviest yarn. Useless. She drew out the needle and began to unravel the work.

"You undo it?" The King had watched Lisel knit and weave and hook for what seemed his entire life. Never had he seen her ravel a work as lovely as what she now pulled apart and wound back on the yarn ball.

"For the Mountain King," she said. "Won't be needed now." She felt strong winding back the yarn on the ball and letting him watch her do it. "What exactly did you want to do for me?"

"Oh, Lisel," he groaned, putting the wine aside to hold his head.

She continued to wind the yarn, letting him find his own way in that dark forest in his head.

"If we had left things as they were...him on his Mountain, us here. Why did we bring him here?"

17

"I have regrets," Lisel said, "but I don't regret my visit there, or his here."

"He loved you," said the King. "He spoke of marrying you."

"Did he?" Lisel wound yarn. "Perhaps I should have done so."

She wound yarn in a way that mesmerized him, watching the work unravel and disappear back into the ball, as if time itself could wind backwards.

"You turned him down?" the King dared surmise.

"I didn't marry him," Lisel said, "but neither did I turn him down."

"How different life would have been, if you and I had married."

"You and I married?" Lisel echoed. "Sitting by the fire on a winter night with half grown children asleep somewhere in this castle?"

He startled, as if she struck him, but all that happened was she stopped protecting him.

"To Lisel, and to her children," the Mountain King had bequeathed his kingdom, "because though you do not dwell on your children, neither do you forget them." Since then, Lisel found herself thinking more often of her children.

"Sons?" he asked with trepidation, as if he saw them mounted and aligned against him.

"One," Lisel replied coolly, sparing him nothing, noting how easy to speak of old losses, now that fresh grief pained her so much more.

"How old?" asked the King as if gauging his

18

enemy.

"I lost count," Lisel dismissed the son, like a dropped stitch in raveled work. She wound off the end of the yarn. "Ask the Chief Steward. He could calculate it for you from his book."

He would never ask the Chief Steward such a thing; they both knew that. He would never have asked Lisel and didn't remember how the conversation turned that direction.

"What is it you want from me?" she asked.

The King sighed, more comfortable on the familiar territory of his needs. "I would like you with me tomorrow, when I tell my Wife about her father."

"She has no fondness for me," Lisel reminded him. "The Chief Steward might be more comfort to her."

"Not to me," he said. "I need you with me. I dread this."

"Very well," said Lisel rising and he rose too, dismissed. "Tomorrow afternoon we will call on her."

Possibly, Lisel thought as she closed the door on him, the shortest encounter with him in their history. She did not want him to start dropping by, to sit at her fire.

She had come to him a few times since his marriage, when he had called for her. He had been as eager as ever, but she found it difficult to resume their former intimacy. She longed for the touch of another man. Tonight would have been impossible. She appreciated that much sensitivity on his part, but saw how on the occasion he tried to comfort her, he begged for her to soothe him. If she had let her care flow towards him, he would have been in her arms, and eventually in her bed. When she sat across the room, patiently waiting to receive his comfort, he had no idea how to deliver such a thing.

If the Mountain King could walk through her door, he would place his hand on her head, smooth her hair and stroke her cheek. He would take her hands, gently open fists clenched against tears and see how her nails cut into the palms. He would hold her. This King she had poured out her life for over the years, sat across the room and did not know how to give compassion. Had he learned notthing from her?

Lisel slept soundly that night. She closed her eyes and saw the woolly fleece of her flop-eared sheep--wool so deep she could not reach the end of it, like the Mountain King's love. She pressed her fingers, arms and whole body into that woolly love and slept, suspended in whiteness where nightmares dared not penetrate.

The King's Wife eagerly anticipated her husband's visit. After the attention of the Grand Parade tour he seemed to have abandoned her. Upon return to the castle she rarely saw him, except from a distance. A group of serving women tended her, but they were keepers rather than company. She could not order them; they took orders from the Chief Steward.

If she asked for something, they checked with him. Sometimes she got what she asked, other times they told her the Chief Steward said later, or he would look into it for her.

The news that her husband planned to call on her in the afternoon sent her into a frenzy of preparation. She kept her women busy all morning, fixing her hair this way and that; going through all the clothes in her cupboard, trying on, discarding, snatching back. She asked for advice, then instantly disregarded it. She arranged herself and rearranged herself, but could not sit still long enough to strike a pose. She kept running to the door to see if he was coming yet.

Her disappointment when she finally saw him mount the stairs, fell like a bucket of cold water over her head. "Why does he bring HER with him?"

The serving women knew why. News of the Mountain King's death, once announced by Tiberius to the King, was set loose among the officers. From there it spread through the castle like a quick hot flame. The King's Wife, of course, they protected from the hot coals of such news.

She saw herself reclining on her sofa, gently rising, floating to meet him, in all her glory. He saw her dash to him and gab his extended hand with both of her hands. The load of ill-matched finery she wore blinded him.

"My dear," he greeted her with a strained smile.

"I am so happy to see you," she cried squeezing his hands. She glared at Lisel and made no acknowledgement of her.

Lisel expected as much and took a seat to the side of the room with the serving women.

The King situated himself where he could see Lisel and drew his Wife to sit by him on the sofa. "I have a grave matter to bring to you."

"Grave? Someone died?" she asked.

His lips parted in a gasp of surprise. Then he saw she tried to make a joke, to flirt with him. "As a matter of fact, yes," he continued, "your father."

"My father?" She blinked as if finding it hard to remember the man. "My father died?"

"He had an accident, on a mountain road." Each word cost the King a bead of perspiration. "Apparently some months ago, but the news just arrived."

"Things like that happen on the Mountain," she said. "Accidents not discovered until later, sometimes spring thaw."

The King began to nervously stroke her hands. "Then you are not so surprised?"

"Well," she said, frowning at the women who hung on her words, "he was old. I might not have seen him again anyway, living here, so far away."

"I had hoped we would see him again," the King said. Easy enough to proclaim now all possibility of doing so was lost.

She looked into his concerned face but did not know what to say. She tried to sound proper. Why did they stare at her so? "What does that mean, for me?"

"I suppose it might mean that you feel sad, or...." The King floundered and looked to Lisel but she did not rush to speak for him.

"I mean," said his Wife more agitated, "do I have to go back to the Mountain and be queen?"

Of all the possible questions and responses he did not expect that one. "Is that what you want?"

"NO!" she cried flinging herself at him, "NO! I never want to go there again. Please don't send me back."

At least he could offer reassurance about that matter. "I have no intention of sending you anywhere. Your life here will not change, and you will not be given responsibility for the Mountain."

She leaned against him and relaxed a bit, but did not let go of him. "I don't want to go there, but I wouldn't mind being Queen here."

He decided to smile and take that as one of her jokes. "There's no need of that either." He straightened her to sit a little more apart from him. "I wanted to tell you myself and determine what kind of mourning you think most appropriate."

"Morning?"

"Mourning." The King turned to Lisel, a bit desperately. "Perhaps Lisel will explain what we do in a period of mourning."

"Oh, manners and stuff," said his Wife.

"Mourning is respect shown for the dead," Lisel said, "so yes, I suppose it is a type of manners."

"And special clothes?" She recalled her father

23

wearing his doeskins on the occasion he buried his
second wife, the same doeskins he recently wore to
her wedding.

"Sometimes, if there's a burial, but since we don't
have his body there won't be a burial, so I don't see
need for new clothes," Lisel said.

"Oh," she sounded disappointed. "What
happened to his body?"

"We were told," Lisel said, "he went over a cliff,
a long way down into a chasm."

"That happens on the Mountain," the girl said.
"He was always telling me to be careful--then it
happens to him."

"Mourning," Lisel said, "is a time we stop other
activities to remember the dead and heal our grief."

"How long?" she asked.

"Grief may take from a year to a lifetime, but
mourning is a symbolic time, usually a few months."

"But it's already been a few months," the girl
quickly returned. "How many do we have left, for
stopping activities?"

"I presume," Lisel said turning to the King, "that
is what the King came to discuss with you."

"But I don't KNOW," she wailed. "I don't know
how many I'm supposed to do, or how many are
already done, or what activity to stop. Nothing
happens anyway. What am I supposed to stop doing?
Getting up and getting dressed in the morning?"

The King shook her slightly. "Stop. You don't
have to decide. We'll ask the Chief Steward. He's very

good at figuring out these things."

The King's Wife let out a long disconsolate sigh. Her anticipated pleasant afternoon with her husband turned into another discussion of manners and unpleasant details, about her father of all people, and death of all the odd topics.

"Can I can do anything for you?" the King asked her, "to make you feel better?"

"Yes," she said, gripping his hands. "I want you to stay with me, and eat dinner with me, and be with me tonight, alone." She glared at the company of women in the corner.

"Very well," said the King. Though he loathed the prospect he could say nothing else under the circumstances.

"Now," she demanded.

"Shortly," he bargained. "I have a few things I must attend, but I will return for dinner and spend the night with you."

"Alone."

"Alone," he agreed. "In the meantime, perhaps you'd like Lisel's company?"

"Why?"

Good question, thought Lisel.

"You might want to talk to her about mourning?"

"I thought you said the old man would take care of that?" she asked. How rude "old man" sounded on her lips, though his intimates affectionately used the nickname.

"He will," Lisel said quickly, "and I'll take the

matter up with him. Immediately, if you'd like that?"

"Yes, do," said the King with a sigh.

The Chief Steward had already calculated the possibilities and impossibilities of mourning for the Mountain King. He proposed no announcement to raise the issue where it need not be raised. Since the Mountain King was not of their Court, there need be no official grieving period. However, as he was related by marriage, and known by some of the Court, his death should be mourned for whatever period deemed appropriate by the individuals in mourning. They were to be respected in their grief, but mourning would not be imposed on those who did not feel so moved by the death. Thus the King's Wife could be excused a long ordeal by counting the time since his death and Lisel could count time from the moment of her knowledge.

The Chief Steward then discussed notifying the Court at Reminnia of the death of a King. "Really, not our business to pass the news," he said pacing one way. "On the other hand, because he was your Wife's father, therefore related--however briefly--we do have some responsibility. Not to send notification, so they can mourn, lacks respectability."

The King vacillated between wanting to be respected by the Reminnian Court and not wanting to be asked difficult questions by them. He grumbled that the worst service Tiberius had done in this affair was reporting the accident. If they didn't know, they wouldn't be responsible. As his Wife said, accidents happen on the Mountain. They wouldn't have known until spring when Lisel took her proposed trip up the Mountain. He put off deciding what, when and if of a message to Reminnia. Enough that he must comfort his Wife that night.

The Chief Steward invited Lisel to share dinner with him that evening.

"I have commenced mourning," she declined, "and prefer to take my meals alone for the duration." She could not abide the thought of eating in the presence of those who dispensed with the crime and the death by the easiest calculated path. If she had any faith in the Reminnian Court, she would have pressed for notification to be sent, so that someone, beside herself, would ask hard questions. From her present perspective she could not imagine why the Reminnians would care. She thought they would only toss condolences toward his daughter, who seemed to care the least.

Perhaps, Lisel thought on her way to her chamber alone, *she was as relieved to be rid of him as he of her.* She recalled how she had been relieved at the death of her long ailing mother. As for her father, his death among many violent deaths at the time she keenly felt. Neither of those losses were so isolating as facing the emptiness of the world without the Mountain King and with no one to share the grief. The bleakness of the world and her lonely position

27

attacked as suddenly as a bandit springing off a boulder. Her measure of composure had been spent for one afternoon. She quickened her step to get safely out of sight before tears overcame her again.

The King refreshed and made himself attractive before returning to his Wife. He found her more subdued than earlier in the day. The high tension of the morning, her disappointment in his earlier visit, followed by the news about her father, left her looking rather forlorn. She sat on the sofa where they sat earlier that day, overdressed, but no longer eager. She would not have been surprised if he sent word he could not come to her after all. When he arrived and dismissed the serving women, to be alone as she requested, she sat, not knowing what to do with him.

The King took charge, adjusting the lamp to a softer glow, which suited him better. He took his Wife's hand, covered with rings and bracelets, and began to slip off the ornaments.

She did not resist, only said rather sadly, as if he took them away forever, "I liked them."

"I like them too," he said, "each one is very nice, but I also like taking them off you." Her hand, stripped of the heavy ornaments, he found to be a pretty little hand and he gently held it.

Without a word she offered him her other hand.

From that one too, he removed each ring and bracelet. Though his thought had been only to quench her discordant appearance before dinner, he now removed each piece with ritual care, placing it on the table. She sat perfectly still, spellbound, while he undid the clasps of the necklaces and removed them from her neck. Off came her earrings and he massaged the red pinch marks on her ear lobes. Then he began undoing the combs in her hair. As her hair tumbled down, he ran his hands through it to search out hidden pins. She gave a little shiver of delight. Sitting quietly, with her hair falling down over her shoulders, she looked more beautiful than he recalled. With unexpected pleasure, he began to unlatch the brooches attached to her bodice. When those were removed, and placed on the growing heap of jewelry on the table, he unhooked the front of her dress.

She gave a deep sigh as he lifted her breasts out of what had felt like a cage all day. He examined each of them, as if jewels, and then gave each a kiss.

Smiling now, pleased he had stumbled upon a game which kept her so quiet, he unhooked her skirt and let his hands in to explore her smooth neat waist.

His Wife shook the loosened dress off her shoulders, freeing her arms. She reached for him and quickly undid the buttons on his vest. When she slipped her hands inside to touch his bare chest, she saw the light of pleasure in his eyes and felt the hesitation of surprise in his fingers playing around her waist.

While the hot supper left by the serving women grew cold on the table, the King and his Wife slowly, with great care, explored each other's bodies in the minutest details. Without saying a word, but with eyes wide open, they surprised themselves by consummating their marriage.

The King's Wife, though she had carefully watched men and women while traveling through the lusty celebrations at Grand Parade, had seen nothing to match what she glimpsed of herself and her husband in the glass on her dressing room door. So entranced was she with the process, and delighted with the sight of his body, especially the sight of it connected to her own, that the moment of penetration elicited only a quick involuntary gasp.

Eventually the fire died down, both at the grate and in their bodies, leaving them shivering. The King wrapped his Wife in a bed shawl, rather than the gaudy clothes.

"Our supper got cold," she observed with a little sniff.

The King sent for another supper and stirred up the coals in the grate himself. His Wife didn't care how many serving women came now to clear and re-set their supper. She hoped they would gossip all night, and all next week, about the glorious state of undress in which they saw the King and his Wife, and how late they dined.

The King watched his Wife eat. She curled in the chair as if a child, wrapped in the shawl which slipped off her shoulders as she reached for her food. She preferred to eat with her fingers and, in this moment of mellow pleasure, forgot the newly learned manners of fork and knife. Watching her, he observed skill in the way she ate with her fingers; adroitly taking small pieces of food and frequently, neatly, licking clean her fingers. So fascinated did he become with the process that, as the supply of finger size bites diminished, he reached across and cut more for her with his own knife and fork.

His Wife froze with the food in her fingers. "I forgot--the fork."

"I suppose it wouldn't do at a great banquet," he said with a smile, "but between us, eat as you please."

They never engaged much conversation. On the Grand Parade tour they made formal appearances and repeated the marriage ceremony four times. The King felt humiliated each time he went through that sham which reminded of his failure to consummate the marriage on the wedding night. Dutifully, as man and wife, they shared quarters but had not attempted to touch each other in an intimate manner. Now, on a night the King felt he must converse in condolences to his Wife, or at least make pleasant conversation with her, they suddenly accomplished the impossible.

After a second glass of wine, his Wife fell asleep at the table. He carried her to her bed and then stood, watching her sleep. A strange, pretty little girl, she appeared, when quiet. If only she could be like this always. He covered her and blew out the lamp. He had promised to spend the night with her and though tempted to tiptoe away to his own quarters, he decided to sleep on the sofa in her outer chamber

How strange, he thought, on a night he should have been consoling her over her father's death, they made love, as if neither had a care in the world. He felt a little guilty now, though at the moment, it seemed the right thing to do. Indeed, the act compelled him, but how strange.

He recalled the death of his own father. He had been about her age, but a great deal more upset by it. Of course, his father's death had been violent and he had seen it happen. Even these many years later, he preferred not to remember it. He could not imagine making love to anyone then. Only a boy, he knew no woman to make love with then. He met Lisel later--- actually, not much later. Although it seemed a long time, when he calculated he realized it wasn't long after the death of his father, and mother, and sisters that he began to desire Lisel.

Perhaps, though he could not think it through, he felt there may be some connection between death and love. The passion of the two chases each other in an eternal circle, driving the world forward.

He thought of his Wife and how her desire for him, made him strong and confident in his lovemaking that night. Once Lisel made him feel strong. He loved her and admired her so deeply that the idea she loved him enhanced him in his own eyes. Since his marriage he felt Lisel had only been tolerating him. She said she expected him to turn his Wife.

The King wanted to share with Lisel the joy of consummating his marriage, marvel with her at the difference in his lovemaking. Then he remembered-- he had never confessed to Lisel that he did not consummate the marriage on the wedding night.

Why, he wondered, did love making seem incomplete unless he included Lisel in some way? She, he recognized, had gone into mourning. He had watched her wrap herself in a cloak of grief and take her leave as clearly as she left the castle for her walk yesterday. He would be left to his own devices with his Wife for awhile.

At least, he thought as he yawned, *tonight turned out surprisingly well*. He had only to sleep on the sofa until dawn. Then he'd be free to return to his own life.

Lisel preferred to remove herself from the castle as often as possible. A few days after her first visit to Danny, she packed a big basket of fresh bread and jam and other delicacies from the castle to carry to him. However, she knew she must stay alert to developments at Court. The question the King's Wife raised about governance of the Mountain warned Lisel she must protect her realm from further interference. Heavy winter weather would prevent traffic that direction for some months, but the subject would be discussed around the winter fire.

The King preferred not to address, more often than necessary, the embarrassing death of the

Mountain King. He never decided what should be said to the Reminnian Court; thus no word went to them. The Chief Steward fussed, but quit pressing the matter. Tiberius had his own plans about Reminnia, too, and they did not hinge on whether their Queen and Twin Kings knew of the death of the Mountain King.

The Mountain came up again when the census books were examined to determine the number of youth coming of age in each province that year.

"How will we count the mountain people?" the Chief Steward inquired. Census taking was relatively simple in the provinces as they were brought under control, one by one. The accessible roads and eagerness of the people to return to organized civil life made it a tedious but not impossible task. "The place is treacherous and they must live in caves in the sides of the mountains. I saw not one house or village there."

"How many do you suppose they number?" the King asked.

The Chief Steward shook his head. "Actually only saw two, plus a couple of wild children."

"His man Silas," the King counted.

"And a woman--his wife, I suppose and probably their children." The Chief Steward turned to Lisel who sat to the side of the room, weaving as usual. She saw more of the Mountain on that trip and had been privy to the Mountain King's trust.

"Maybe there aren't any more," she said.

"One family?" the King cried. "Incredible!"

The Chief Steward jolted because he thought it quite possible. "Possibly one family is alone, in those terrible mountains. Should we send assistance?"

"Silas," Lisel said firmly, "has lived on the Mountain all his life without our assistance, and he knows the way here if he wants help."

"True," said the King. "I don't think it's a matter of assistance, but there must be more people. My Wife would know."

He sent for his Wife who arrived in a dither without time to overdress as elaborately as she wished.

"I don't know how many people," she whined. "They run like little ants under the rocks whenever you want one."

This matched the Chief Steward's perception of the worthlessness of the Mountain. They already had more mountain sheep and goats than he wanted. He had dispersed them to the provinces hoping they would blend and disappear. Mountain people might be more problematic than sheep.

Lisel privately recalled how quickly the women helping Hannah in the kitchen disappeared that night she tried to join them. The girl likely spoke the truth and obviously she did not care about the people.

"Should we bring them down to a better life?" asked the King.

The King's Wife did not want the mountain people to arrive in her new life. She disdained them even when they were the only people, other than her father, in her world. "No," she said. "They'd be of no use to you. Besides, you'd never catch them. They hide in holes and rocks, worthless."

The King felt relieved he would not be expected to do anything about the mountain people. The whole affair aroused a vague guilt and irritated him. Why should he feel guilty because the Mountain King had an accident? He had not cause it. The guilt seemed to run deeper, around the initial disturbance of those ants on the Mountain and for bringing a Wife he did not want into his Court. He had acquired the Mountain, so it appeared, and found it worthless.

"I wouldn't mind," announced his Wife into his silence, "if I woke up one morning and looked out and the mountains were gone--GONE!" She swung her arm, as if to level them and would have swept the lamp off the table if the Chief Steward had not rescued it. "I would like to wake up one morning and find the world on the back side of the castle, looks exactly like the front side--more plains and provinces-- like a looking glass." She smiled coyly at the King and with one of her surprisingly quick and unexpected movements, threw herself into his lap. "All yours."

The shocked King, embarrassed by the way she fondled him before the others, set her back on her feet. "I doubt we can level the mountains into plains to please you, my dear," he said, trying to smile, "but it does appear we have no reason to worry about the people there."

Lisel and the Chief Steward made no complaint about this decision, and offered no further questions, so the King thanked his Wife and dismissed her. She looked disappointed at not being invited to stay longer in his company, but took her leave when the door was opened for her.

Tiberius had remained silent through this discussion. Now he said, "the people may be worthless but I'd like to find the horses."

"The horse went over the cliff," the Chief Steward reminded him.

"He had more," Tiberius insisted.

"Ah yes, the white and the gray."

"More than those," Tiberius said. "I am sure, and since the people present no threat, I'll take a scouting party next spring to hunt for them."

Lisel felt her blood rise. As Queen of the Mountain she must not let that happen, but had no army to stop him. She did not even have a way to get up the Mountain ahead of him to warn the people, if she could find them. Horses or no horses, the vision of Tiberius ravaging the Mountain hunting for them upset her.

"I suppose," mused the King, "it won't matter."

"I think it matters a great deal," Lisel said," if you have any concern about the proximity of the Mountain King's death to his daughter's wedding."

The King shifted in his chair. He had a great deal of uneasiness about that unfortunate coincidence.

"It would not make the matter look any better to so quickly acquire his horses, whether two or two hundred."

"We would look like horse thieves?" the King asked, slightly amused.

Tiberius snorted, more amused.

"Nothing can be done until Spring," said the Chief Steward, with a glance toward Lisel, "and that is some time away. Let us deal with matters at hand, the quota of youth for the year."

That topic interested Tiberius as much as horses. He settled into haggling for the outrageous number of men he wanted for troops in the coming year, but did not forget Lisel's implied accusation.

"So," he teased, catching her by the door, as she left them to their evening meal, "you call me a horse thief?"

She disengaged her arm. "I called you nothing."

"I'll say this," he replied, "if I'd killed a man for his horse, I'd come back with the horse."

"You were on Grand Parade," she returned, "as we all know." She had no intention to discuss the matter with him, but took the opportunity to raise the King's suspicions. "Your man, Jurgius, however, may not be so clever as you."

The King overheard exactly as she planned. "You think Jurgius did not give a true report of all he knows?"

"I," she replied, "never heard Jurgius' report, nor have you. We heard a second hand report."

"We shall hear from him," the King decided. "Tomorrow, Tiberius, bring him to us. I have a few questions myself."

Tiberius shrugged, "as you please." He then excused himself from dining with the King and the Chief Steward and left the room with Lisel. They turned opposite directions in the passageway without a backward glance to each other.

Jurgius, a senior officer, arrived at the King's Court the next morning as commanded. Though younger, Lisel observed that he resembled Tiberius. All the officers resembled him in some sense. This one, Jurgius, had the same hard dark eyes, but no hint of the humor that often played in Tiberius' face. Even now, Tiberius settled himself to enjoy the encounter between this senior officer and the assembled Court.

The Chief Steward avoided officers; Lisel encountered them primarily when wounded and they required her aid. Neither recognized Jurgius. Nor did the King know him, though he had ridden in battle and knew many officers by name.

Jurgius took his time unhooking his winter gray cloak. He seemed in no hurry to begin this matter but did not appear under the duress, as if on trial. He gave his report in a few short sentences. He had been ordered by Tiberius to follow the Mountain King as far as his gate, but to keep a distance because the Mountain King preferred to travel alone. He did so, and observed on a narrow place in the road, the horse took a step, close to the edge of the road. The edge gave way and the Mountain King and his horse went over the cliff. When he arrived at the place to look down, he saw a long, impossibly long, way below in the rocks the horse and the man lay dead. Since Tiberius had been reviewing troops in the western provinces until recently, he had not given his report earlier.

The Chief Steward, busy writing down every word, and checking back over his pages, asked many questions to get the report straight. He felt this might be the best opportunity to make a sensible report to send the Reminnian Court, which must be done, the sooner the better.

"What did you understand to be your purpose in following him?"

"To observe him," Jurgius replied, "because it was dangerous for him to travel alone."

"Yet, you traveled alone, or did you have others with you?"

Jurgius looked to Tiberius, but finding no cue, he said, "I traveled alone."

"Not so dangerous for you then, eh?" asked the Chief Steward.

"I am younger and do not drink on the road."

"Ah, yes the drink," recalled the Chief Steward. "Did you see the Mountain King drinking?"

"Yes sir. He carried a jug and he drank from it."

"And you were close enough," the King asked,

"that you could see he drank wine, not water?"

"The jug, sir," Jurgius chose his words carefully, "was of the type normally used to carry wine, though I was not close enough to see what came out of it."

"Then you only guess he drank wine?" asked the King, who had taken a dislike to this man associated with an unpleasant topic.

"I surmised," said Jurgius, "because he rode slumped in the saddle and because he was reported to drink heavily, and not water, it must be wine."

The Chief Steward stroked his chin, considering the matter. He did not recall the Mountain King riding slouched. He could not visualize such a thing. "How many jugs of wine did he carry?"

"I did not count, sir."

"So many?" cried the Chief Steward. "I recall him leaving with a fair sized pack to the rear of his horse, but wine jugs are bulky. So many, you could not count?"

"Did not, sir," Jurgius said tersely, "not, could not."

"Why not?" asked the King. "If you observed him drinking, and increasing his danger, and knew you were to report to Tiberius, would not the matter of how much he drank be important?"

"I saw only the jug from which he drank."

"Then," calculated the Chief Steward who was very quick at calculating supplies, "there must have been only one. And you say the accident occurred on the high narrow part of the road. That part comes at least two days into the journey. Therefore, one jug of wine spread over two days would not make a man drunk." He did not mean to offer defense of the Mountain King, only to make his report as clear as possible.

"I do not know," said Jurgius, "that it was the same jug."

"Did you see him finish one and open another?" asked the King.

"No sir."

"Then he only had one, or you did not have him in your observation at all times?"

Jurgius again looked to Tiberius, but received no help; he continued on his own. "In the dark, at night, he could have changed jugs."

"You camped at night, on the road, then?" The Chief Steward continued scribbling in his book.

"Yes sir."

"And slept?" asked the King.

"Yes sir."

The King addressed Tiberius on that issue. "Isn't it unusual to send a man alone on an observation mission that will take more than one day, with no one to spell the watch?"

Tiberius shrugged, "an unusual mission."

"Indeed," agreed the King, "but why only one man?"

"We were not at war with the Mountain King," said Tiberius, "only a gesture of help."

"But if the Mountain King broke camp in the

night, while your officer slept, he would lose him."

"Not likely," said Tiberius, "on that singular road, and why would the Mountain King break camp in the middle of the night when he doesn't know he's being followed?"

"Wait!" cried the Chief Steward waving his pen. "How can it be a gesture of help, to send a man along behind, if he doesn't know the help is there?"

"A party of soldiers," Tiberius explained patiently to the old man, "would appear threatening. One man, seen only if he needs help, is a gesture of help."

"But, alas" sighed the Chief Steward, "so far behind, he didn't turn out to be any help."

No, thought the King with annoyance, *only created the inconvenience of his report*

"The accident, sir," Jurgius took up the report again, "happened so quickly, that even had I been a few paces behind, I doubt I could have helped him without going over myself."

"Start over again, please," asked the Chief Steward, dipping his pen.

"He rode slumped in his saddle..."

"What time of day?" snapped the Chief Steward.

"Oh, mid day," Jurgius said, as if it did not matter, "and the horse appeared to weave, stepping perilously close to the edge of the road..."

"The horse appeared to weave?" Lisel interrupted.

They all turned; surprised to hear her voice, as if

they forgot she sat working at her loom.

"Yes," Jurgius with irritation at being questioned by a woman.

"Do you say the horse was drunk?" she asked.

"No," said Jurgius, with a patronizing smile, "but a drunk man riding a horse can cause the horse to veer, with improper direction and reining."

"I rode many times with the Mountain King," Lisel said, sending the shuttle back on the loom resuming her work. "He did not use a rein. He would say, 'Home, Blazer' and the horse would take him straight there, even if he fell asleep in the saddle."

"I was to the rear," Jurgius said.

"You observed a man ride for how many days and did not see if he used a rein?" asked the King, less impressed every minute with this officer.

"I observed the horse weaving, so presumed that he reined improperly, but the lady may be correct as I also observed he used his hands freely to raise the jug," Jurgius replied.

"And did he also offer the jug to the horse?" asked Lisel, "and to his dog, Rufus? He was fond of them, shared all his food. "

"I did not observe that," Jurgius replied.

"But the horse," repeated the Chief Steward as he wrote, "did weave on the road?"

"And stepped near the edge and went over." Jurgius said attempting to mark the end of the report.

"You saw him go over," the King said, "and you saw the body of the man and the horse below?"

"Yes, sir."

"Are you certain he was dead? Did you go down to offer help?"

"Impossible! Such a long way down, I could scarcely see them and even if I got down, I could never get up again."

"A treacherous road," agreed the Chief Steward, "I've seen it myself."

"How long did you observe to make sure he did not move, or call for help?" asked the King.

"It was late in the day," Jurgius began.

"Mid day," prompted the King.

"Yes, but later by the time I arrived," Jurgius qualified. "I watched until dark."

"And then?" asked the Chief Steward eager for new tidbits.

"Dark, and the road so treacherous in that place, I dared not move. I camped and..." Jurgius paused, then added with the delight of discovering a good invention, "I looked over again in the morning and found the bodies as they lay the night before."

"Why," asked the King, moved to explore the bad judgement of this man, "did you wait all afternoon, evening and night in such a treacherous place, after determining you could be of no assistance?"

"To make a full and complete report, sir."

"Because report, rather than assistance, was the purpose of your mission?" The King felt disgust for this officer.

"As I recall, my order was to observe and report on his journey."

The King dismissed the report. "I have no further questions." He gestured to the others. "Lisel?"

"Where is the dog?" she asked.

"The dog?" asked Jurgius, caught off guard as surely as if Rufus crept from under Lisel's skirt to bite him.

"Rufus always traveled by his side."

Jurgius had no ready answer.

"You left me with a picture of the horse and the man going over the cliff, but the dog still stands in the road in my mind," Lisel pressed. "Was he there when you arrived, to look over the cliff?"

"No," said Jurgius.

"What happened to him?" Lisel asked.

"Maybe he went over too," said Jurgius.

"Rufus?" Lisel cried. "How could that happen?"

"I don't know that it did," Jurgius back tracked, "but maybe it jumped, if so devoted it followed everywhere."

The Chief Steward frowned. "Dogs have been noted for devotion to men, especially that one, but I don't recall any account of a dog jumping off a cliff after a man."

"Nor do I," said the King, "though I know little about dogs." *However, I do know something about men and this one is either lying or stupid*, he thought to himself.

"I would assume," Lisel said, looking Jurgius in

46

the eye until he averted his face from her gaze, "Rufus would stay at the spot in the road where the accident occurred, quite frantic."

"Maybe ran away," Jurgius said with irritation.

"Not likely," said Lisel, "unless frightened away, and Rufus never seemed easy to scare."

"Only a dog," Tiberius interrupted. "Any number of things could have happened Maybe he tried to go down to them, before Jurgius arrived."

"Maybe," said Lisel. "I think Rufus would try to get to him, no matter how far he fell, but how strange you did not see the dog below, if you watched all afternoon and evening."

Jurgius made no reply since he had not been asked a direct question. He stood staring straight ahead, waiting to be dismissed. Tiberius let him stand an unbearably long time, then dismissed him, when the others did not ask more questions.

"Well?" Tiberius inquired, pacing about the King's workroom, in the silence after Jurgius' departure. "Well?"

"Certainly not a man of good judgement," the King observed.

Tiberius bristled but neither defended nor agreed.

"Odd, about the dog." The Chief Steward tapped his cheek with the pen. "And, I do recall now, the Mountain King did not use a rein. Frightened me half to death that day we rode about the mountains. He sat and gestured, here and there, and let the horse find its own way."

"In places with no roads," Lisel added.

"And the other two horses followed, quite sure footed, though I felt certain we would all be lost," the Chief Steward recalled.

"The road up the Mountain, even at its narrowest would be a grand highway to Blazer," Lisel said.

"So do you accuse my man of a crime?" Tiberius asked. "Do you think he killed the Mountain King?"

"I don't see how one man, as stupid as that one," said the King, "could overcome the Mountain King mounted on that great horse. No, I think he reports an accident, but has poor judgement. Nor did he take to heart the true meaning of his mission, to be of help in danger."

"Then we are not horse thieves?" Tiberius teased with a grin, "only clumsy fools?"

"I am not amused by the accident or the report," the King snapped. He turned to the Chief Steward, pondering his pages of writing, making corrections with dots and crossings. "Tear up that report."

"Tear up my report?" cried the Chief Steward.

"Enter in the book only that the death of the Mountain King was reported to us on a particular day last week."

The Chief looked disappointed. He loved his reports

"I want no record of that embarrassing escort or excuse for a report in the book." The King chose stupidity, rather than lies, to dismiss this difficult matter.

"Yes, sir." The Chief Steward tore the pages from the book, but folded them and put them inside his robes. He made the entry as requested by the King and read it back for approval.

The King looked to Lisel who quit weaving. He watched her cover her loom and take her leave without a word. He dared not ask if she accepted the report. The matter had only been made worse by investigation. He resolved not to have it spoken of again.

Following Jurgius' report Lisel found it difficult to cling to the vision of endless wool in sleep. Unwelcome dreams punctuated her nights. She saw Rufus falling, legs akimbo, long ears flying as he rolled over and over, falling through blue sky. Though she managed to wake herself and sit bolt upright with heart pounding before the image of the dog smashed on the rocks, she felt certain that Rufus went over the cliff. She felt equally certain he did not jump, though how he went, she could not fathom. Other times, when she let go of the wool in her sleep, she saw the Mountain King dead, face down at the bottom of a chasm. Again, her mind, which resisted these images, spared her the fall, spared her the dead face, but she saw his body, splayed and dead, in a deep canyon. At that image she would wake and feel, not the terror of seeing Rufus tumble through space, but her heart breaking with pain so severe she must double over to hug her breasts as she wept.

The horse, Blazer, she could not find in her nightmares. No stretch of irrational imagination could conjure, even to torment her, the image of Blazer falling over a cliff. The entire road would have to cave in under him to bring such an event. As she recalled the road, hacked into the side of the Mountain, that did not seem reasonable. Traveling in her mind, up and down, recalling a trip she remembered well, she could not find one place with the edge of the road in danger of giving way.

Once wakened by these nightmares, Lisel found it impossible to return to sleep. She would rise, make a hot brew to drink and knit to let her mind try to make sense of the matter, as her fingers made sense of the threads running deftly between them. Some things she could deduce. If the Mountain King went over the cliff, but Blazer did not, he had been off the horse when he met his adversary. Why, in a moment of danger, did he dismount? No one could pull him off that horse without being trampled. Had he dismounted to open the gate? Unlikely--the latches were high, she recalled, probably for exactly that reason. Lisel could made no sense of those thought threads and often discovered by daylight she chose to tear out the knitting done while considering them. The toll of sleepless nights began to show in her face. The mark of mourning settled on Lisel's face and required no dark veil to announce her grief.

The King felt consternation as he watched her

fade. He blamed himself for allowing that idiot, Jurgius, to report in court. Obviously the officer bungled the job he had been sent to do and made a worse mess of the report.

Tiberius left the castle for his winter inspection of the Eastern Provinces. Before he left he promoted Jurgius to Castle Fort Commander.

Though the King never interfered in Tiberius' management of his officers, he grumbled when Tiberius announced Jurgius' promotion. "I hope no emergency occurs."

"Fear no emergencies," Tiberius laughed and slapped him on the back before leaving for the Eastern Provinces.

The King, a fit warrior himself, would not rely on Jurgius in an emergency. He would take the command himself, but nothing would happen. Peace in the provinces had been accomplished. Peace in his household presented a more pressing problem that winter. Lisel faded with grief and his Wife made mischief in her boredom.

After the visit to Lisel's chamber, where he felt himself an intruder and rather quickly dismissed the King chose not to go there again. He called for her one night, but before he could explain he wanted nothing more than to comfort her, she spoke to him.

"I came because you called, but I am in mourning and have nothing to give you."

"Lisel, Lisel," he begged "is there nothing I can offer to comfort you?"

"What would that be?" she asked, frankly meeting his gaze.

He found himself the emptiest of men with nothing to give the woman he loved most. "Perhaps only relief from my demands," he replied, hoping to hear her reassure him of his worthiness.

"Thank you," she replied. "I will make good use of my solitude."

He could do nothing but let Lislel go and refrain from calling her again. He turned more to his Wife. He devised more games to entertain her, and though they also amused him for the moment, he found no lasting satisfaction in them, or with her.

The Chief Steward worried, too. Always in the habit of calling on Lisel, he continued to do so.

"How long will you grieve, Lisel?" he begged as winter wore on and he saw no change in her face.

"How long does grief for a lost lover require?" she countered. "How long did you grieve losing me?"

The Chief Steward had never fully recovered; not even today could he declare his grief cured. "A long while."

"With me still alive."

He nodded. Of course, his loss of her was not so terrible as a death, but terrible in other ways.

"Do not worry," she comforted him, for she felt more friendly compassion for him than for the King, "I don't care to sit as often with you and him, but I have been busy."

"What have you been doing?" he inquired,

grasping the thread of conversation as he caught the yarn ball rolling off her lap.

"I spend a fair amount of time out with Danny and the sheep. He has half a dozen mountain dowry sheep, plus my own flop-eared babe."

The Chief Steward smiled, though he wished she had found an occupation not to remind her of the Mountain.

"I may go out to stay awhile at lambing time. Danny thinks they will come later than ours."

"Why?" asked the Chief Steward, allowing her to use his hands to wind yarn, and keep her chatting in his presence.

"What he observes and what the Mountain King said makes sense; Spring comes later on the Mountain." Her eye traveled out the window, to the mountains buried in snow.

The Chief Steward realized he could wind wool until they ran out of sheep and not distract her thoughts from the Mountain King. He continued to call on her though, for he continued to love her no matter who came between them. Meanwhile he observed how the King spent more time with his Wife. One day, one year, Lisel would resolve the grief of her brief affair with the Mountain King and find him still devoted to her. A lifetime would not be too long to wait, as long as no harm befell her. That she remained alive and nearby always comforted him.

The days Lisel felt most relief from grief were those she packed a basket of food and trudged out to visit Danny. As the days grew longer, she started earlier and stayed later. With shared excitement they observed the thick wool of the mountain sheep. They delighted how devoted the flop-eared ewe stayed. She wouldn't lamb this year, too young, Danny said

The other mountain ewes were all expectant and Danny watched them with a careful eye. They'd be difficult, because as much attention as he and Lisel lavished on them, they remained wild and wary. Danny didn't want to lose any, as much for Lisel's sake as for the sheep. He didn't discourage her from planning to stay with him for the lambing. Instead, he made repairs on his shack to better accommodate her. His sisters, who came from the provinces at lambing time, did not care much for these new sheep. They reported problems with them in the provinces, but at least they bred with the local sheep. Perhaps in a generation or two they might blend.

Danny prepared for lambing by trimming around the udders and docks on the pregnant ewes. He reinforced the shelter of the lambing shed and repaired the slatted panels he used each year for birthing pens. By the time Lisel arrived, with a small bundle of clothes, to stay for the duration, Danny and his sisters were filling the pens with deep straw, and keeping an eye on the ewes for signs of labor.

The cold wind, the early spring mud and rain, and bleating of sheep cleared Lisel's senses better than any activity in the castle those months. Sleeping in the rough shack, or taking her turn with Danny while the sisters slept, reminded her of childhood. She had no nightmares about falling dogs and dead kings during lambing season.

Danny had a wise eye for his sheep. He knew which ones needed to be moved to the lambing pens, often before Lisel or his sisters suspected. He had a sense of timing, as if his own body moved in rhythm with their labors. He knew when to leave them be, and when with a grunt, almost a baaing sound himself, to move among them or give one of the women a nod, towards a ewe in need of assistance.

Wrestling, with tears drawn by the cold, arms aching, to hold a distressed ewe for Danny, or reaching in herself to turn a lamb presenting breech, or with a turned head, begging from capricious nature a live birth, suited Lisel's mood. The work left no space to think of past or future. The joy of seeing a lamb, head tucked neatly between front legs, coming forth into the world, elated her. Unfolding and tending a newborn lamb, the most critical moment in the newborn's life, demanded all her attention. Not a spec of attention dared wander to her grief. The struggle with life and death, winning and losing, played out over and over, restored her strength.

Danny said, even as they faced exhaustion after a heavy night, in which they lost a ewe, that things could have been worse. Last year it rained so hard the fields flooded. The lambing shed came down in a storm, and they had only makeshift shelter. They slipped and slid, losing lambs, drowned in mud before they could find them. They heard mired ewes they couldn't reach, bleating and dying. They did not have enough hands to tend all the motherless lambs.

This year, Danny declared a good lambing season. His sisters told their worst stories and watched those late blooming mountain sheep, as if the worst might not be over this season.

The mountain ewes remained heavy with lambs after the rest of the flock delivered. Danny's sisters grew restive and he sent them home. He and Lisel, who had proved herself as competent as in her younger days, could finish. The sisters left with ambivalent backward glances. The hardworking women did not like leaving a job unfinished, but they needed to return to their families.

Lisel and Danny had plenty to do; making sure that all the new lambs nursed and the ewes remained healthy. They prepared the lambing shed again, and watched the mountain ewes, which watched them.

The five mountain ewes picked the same night, the same hour, to commence labor. Skittish as they were, and as hard as Danny and Lisel worked, they could not be everywhere at once. Still, they agreed they made the right decision to send the sisters away. Lisel and Danny truly loved these strange sheep. They struggled through the night, hampered by having only lantern light in the shed. Danny never wanted to lose ewes or lambs, and Lisel felt desperately attached to these who had been transplanted, against their will, from the Mountain.

She wondered if they had known the skill of the Mountain King's hand at their last lambing. She still saw them as his sheep, and none could be lost. Nevertheless, one ewe and two lambs were lost.

"Still, not a bad job," Danny insisted to comfort Lisel. "Five lambs, for we've got a set of twins. If the bereaved takes the orphan, it'll turn out not a bad job for the two of us and them."

Lisel despaired over losing any. The sight of the dead ewe overwhelmed her. Danny let her sit on a rock and cry, as if he sensed she cried for more than one lost sheep. He dragged the carcass out of view and covered it. Later, he'd skin it and save that sheep skin for her. Next time she came, he'd have it clean and dry and soft for her. She'd welcome it, though the sight now broke her heart.

The bereaved sheep refused the orphan, in spite of Danny's seasoned tricks to fool her. Perversely, she kidnapped one of the twins. Danny and Lisel watched, but let the mothers work it out among themselves. When they were arranged, four ewes and four lambs, with no room for the orphan, Lisel decided to take the motherless lamb home with her.

"Like last year, with my flop-eared friend," she said. "I'll enjoy another babe this year." The flop-eared sheep shook her head and flapped its noisy ears as if she not could imagine why those other silly sheep wanted to bother with lambs.

Lisel wrapped her orphan in a blanket and carried it close to her breast, safe out of the wind.

"Shearing next," she said to Danny as he walked with her as far as the road.

Danny nodded.

"Save the fleece from my flop-eared," she requested.

"I thought you'd be out to do the job yourself?"

"I could," Lisel decided, looking back where sheep with new lambs dotted the hillside.

"Those sheep won't like being sheared by strangers any better than lambing with strangers," he said. "I thought I'd do them early and not take them down to the shearing barns."

"And this little one will be ready to wean by then. I'll come," Lisel decided. "You think we can do them, by ourselves?"

"By us or the thing won't be done," Danny said. "These sheep got such a reputation, nobody wants their wool bad enough to wrestle them."

"I want it," Lisel decided. She felt thin spring sun on her face--the end of bitter winter.

Walking home, carrying the lamb, she searched for the image of wool that protected her sleep. She tested it in the fingers of her mind and found it strong. She would have real wool soon between her fingers, to spin and weave.

The King and the Chief Steward saw it as a good sign when Lisel returned from lambing in good spirits. They shook their heads, but smiled at her

58

orphan. Something made her smile again, even if not at them. Her friends among the castle service began to come by to visit, finding Lisel apparently recovered from mourning. They laughed how she fed the big baby, and how it raised havoc in the castle. No one recalled, aloud, her lamb from last spring, but Lisel happily relived those moments. She saw this funny looking, oversized lamb as another gift from the Mountain King.

Summer came sooner than Danny predicted after the harsh winter. Lisel watched the weather as shrewdly from her castle window as Danny watched from his shack doorway in the hills. She determined the time correctly--early by most sheep, but suitable for the exceptionally shaggy mountain sheep. Danny could finish and move the others south to the provincial communal shearing barns. With a basket of supplies, and her lamb on a lead, Lisel set out on the familiar path. This lamb could not be trusted to trot at her heels as the flop-eared ewe walked last year. On this fellow she kept a tight leash.

Danny readied for the task by calling one of his nephews, a boy coming of age the next year. Together they sharpened the shearing blades and waited for Lisel.

"I've been gauging the eyes and the size of those sheep," Danny said as they looked over the mountain sheep held in a pen waiting the first shearing. "I doubt I can hold them, alone, but he and I can hold them, if you can shear."

Danny and the youth, well experienced with his father's flock, knew they'd have a tough time with the indignant sheep. While his own sheep trusted him to roll them over, and some even seemed to like having the heavy fleece sheared off, these sheep were not so sure shearing was a good thing.

Danny selected Lisel's flop-eared yearling ewe first. She might be most most amenable to Lisel's clucking and consoling. Danny and his nephew stood by in case she needed help, but to Lisel's delight, her ewe allowed her to take her around the neck, and gently roll her on her back.

"Good girl," Lisel murmured to the nervous ewe.

Lisel sheared, not terribly close. She wanted a quick job for herself and the sheep. Some motions, some actions, learned young and done often, come back the same as words to a song from childhood, not lost through the years. With a sure hand Lisel clipped the wool between the front legs, and the belly wool. The ewe grunted but stayed still as Lisel clipped around her dock, then quickly up to her head. With a sense of excitement, both at the beauty of the fleece and how she managed on her own, Lisel rolled the ewe on her side and with a few long swift strokes, plowed through the fleece, releasing the body as if she snipped off a jacket.

Standing quiet and watchful, repressing the urge to whoop and holler to celebrate success, Danny and his nephew exchanged looks of pride in Lisel's skill. With a bleat, as if to say--enough--the shorn sheep scrambled to her feet. She shook her head, scolded Lisel a moment, then bounded away to get used to her new summer self.

The boy rolled the fleece in a tarp to save it for Lisel, while Danny patted her back. Then, all three looked with sober eyes, at the ram in the pen, which watched them with an adversarial eye. He had seen the shearing, seen that the sheep bounded away unharmed, but did not look convinced.

"Let's go for him while we're still strong," Danny decided, with grim perseverance.

Danny managed to roll the annoyed ram down, and the strong young nephew, held the back legs while Lisel once more moved in with the shears. In spite of all their reassuring words, Danny got nipped and the boy got kicked, when they rolled the ram to the side, but Lisel managed not to nick the ram's skin.

In spite of his lighter coat, the ram did not frolic away like the yearling. Rather, he stalked, glowering, and hid himself as if ashamed to be seen by the ewes.

The shearing team deciding the worst was over: the anticipation, the first one, and the ram. They took a break for a hearty lunch.

In the afternoon they finished the four ewes with varying degrees of animosity, but no serious damage to either sheep or persons.

"I hate to admit," Danny said, though he grinned at the bundles neatly tied and stacked, "how long it took three of us to shear so few sheep."

The boy laughed. "That we sheared them at all

will be a good tale to tell. They won't even try in the provinces. They'll let them go all summer."

"We should travel the provinces to shear them?" suggested Danny.

"I'd go with you, but..." the lad looked shyly to Lisel, "can you spare the time?"

Lisel had no interest in traveling the provinces to shear more sheep. She wanted to take her load of wool and begin to spin and weave. Her fingers tingled at the prospect. "You shear. Let Danny and another good man hold them for you."

"You think I could?"

"You have a gentle hand and good will toward them," she said kindly. She had been impressed how the boy had not become impatient, or rough, even when he took a bruise or a nip from the cross sheep.

"Could we?" begged the boy.

"Somebody should," Danny mused. "Hot for them here in summer, not sheared."

"Might be my last time," the boy pleaded.

Danny's face clouded as he nodded. "We'll do it."

They watched him run off to play with Lisel's ornery little ram lamb, to celebrate his victory. She thought of her own son, raised somewhere in the provinces. Had he grown as tall and strong and good as this boy?

"He comes of age next year," Danny told Lisel.

"And trek comes close to shearing time," Lisel recalled.

Danny nodded. "Look at him. Tiberius will never

let one that fine be a sheepherder."

Lisel agreed but had no heart to say so to Danny who already grieved the loss his nephew.

Danny shook his head, answering his own question, "not now, not when he's rumbling for war."

Lisel looked up sharply. Had she separated herself so thoroughly from the affairs of Court she did not know of impending war? She did not want to confess such ignorance to Danny and he did not explain further what he heard by rumor.

They had more wool from the mountain sheep than Lisel cared to carry back to the castle. She took only the fleece from her flop-eared ewe, which refused to acknowledge her after the indignity of shearing. She urged Danny's nephew to take a load to his mother to knit him some sweaters and socks. Danny did a fair amount of spinning and knitting in his solitary life; he would make good use of that wool, too. The remainder could be sent to the Northeast Province weavers with the other wool.

Lisel insisted she could carry the bundled fleece on her back, though Danny's nephew offered to walk back with her to carry it. Lisel declined. Her walks gave her time for rumination. Danny understood and discouraged the boy from insisting on helping her.

"Thank you, Danny." She gave him a hug.

Danny stepped back, embarrassed but pleased. Her thanks ran deeper than for wool, or care of sheep, but for the healing friendship they shared over the winter. He would move south with the sheep in a few days and she would not see him until next winter.

Lisel walked down the road, with the awkward bundle on her back, slightly bent. She found it not heavy, but hot and tiresome. It forced her to stop and rest from time to time. Remembrance of the satisfying work and good fellowship of the day replaced the dark thoughts that usually descended on her on this long hike. She enjoyed her slow journey into the late afternoon shadows--until she caught sight of a horse at the crossroad to the main castle road.

As if mentioning his name conjured him out of the summer afternoon haze, Tiberius sat on his horse, waiting for her. He seemed in exceptionally good spirits, which reminded Lisel of Danny's comment about war. Nothing pleased Tiberius more than prospect of war.

"Lisel," he greeted her, "I thought I saw an old woman from the provinces lumbering a load of grease wool!"

"Your eyes deceive you less than some of your officers," she returned. "You did see an old woman from the provinces with a load of grease wool. What are you about?"

"No good, by your high standards, I'm sure," he countered, "but I'll give you a lift with that load."

"No thanks," Lisel declined. "I'd prefer not to be seen riding with you."

"I'd rather not be seen carrying a load of grease wool, but I'd do it for you."

She did not want him to touch her precious wool.

"Very well then," he said and thundered off, leaving a cloud of dust so thick she waited until it settled before proceeding on the road.

Later, a soldier met her on the main road with a cart pony on a lead rein.

"A pony, from Tiberius," he announced.

That much she accepted. Afternoon shadows were gaining on her. She put the fleece bundle on the pony's back, but declined his offer to bring the pony in for her.

"You have more important things to do, I am sure," she said, "and I can lead the pony."

With Tiberius back in the castle she must pay attention to Court discussions. The protective white armor of snow on the Mountain would soon recede. If Tiberius still had in mind to hunt for the horses, she knew no way to stop him. Tending sheep and plans for spinning and weaving eased her grief, but accomplished nothing toward protecting the Mountain from the enemy. She felt helpless and foolish for daring to imagine she had capacity to oversee the Mountain. Similar to over estimating her strength at the end of long day of shearing, she felt small and uselessly tired in the face of the mountains. Given time, given a chance to learn from the Mountain King, she might have done well. The opportunity had been jerked away from her as roughly as she stepped into rut in the road, twisting her ankle. Pain swept through her body; she had not been watching as carefully as she should. Grief and loneliness, just when she thought them banished, also rushed over her, knocking her flat with tears of rage at her ineptitude. No serious damage was done to her ankle, but frustration brought tears to her eyes. She could walk; though she knew her ankle would swell and be a bother for several days. She arrived exhausted at the castle gate, nursing the limp, almost forgetting her pleasure in the fleece until she lifted the bag off the pony's back. The springy, almost live, feel of the fleece inside restored her sagging spirits as much as the compress she intended to put on the ankle.

Tiberius did not have mountain horses as much on his mind as Lisel feared. Something else, sighted in the low plains, ignited his interest in the opposite end of the world. Reminnia preyed on his mind.

Lisel sat by during a session listening to him haggle with the Chief Steward over the number of young men he wanted for troops in the next disbursement. Danny's rumors proved correct, but not new.

The Chief Steward, trying to divert Tiberius from Reminnia, reminded him about the mountain horses. Lisel felt betrayed for a moment by the old man. Then she saw how the old manipulator arranged the ploy to her favor by bringing it up before the King.

"No," said the King, rising out of his chair to emphasize his point. "No one is to go up the

Mountain for horses, or anything else."

"Forget the horses," Tiberius said. "They can wait."

"The Mountain King's horses in our possession would look very bad right now," the King continued.

"Why any worse now?" Lisel asked with a trace of cynicism.

"Because I am waiting for reply from the Court at Reminnia."

"You told them about the Mountain King?" Lisel inquired, realizing how far behind in news she fell over the winter.

"Not exactly," said the Chief Steward. "We sent word asking for a meeting with them."

"I thought a meeting better than a message to be misunderstood," the King explained. "We have not yet heard from them."

"They answered," Tiberius said. "They are building a wall."

"A wall?" the other three echoed.

"A stone wall," Tiberius said. "They have been working in secret for over a year."

"How do you know?" quizzed the Chief Steward, "if in secret?"

"Last summer we began to see structures along the border, but they seemed isolated, unrelated, until recently."

"What changed?" asked the King.

"They are connecting them now, under cover of the forests at the edges of the provinces. This winter, while we were not much in the low plains, they started building in several locations there."

"A wall across the entire border? All the way across the low plains?" The King gaped, astounded. "Impossible."

"Not if they keep at it long enough," Tiberius said. "They won't finish this year, maybe not even by next year, but they are, I am certain, building a wall."

"Why?" asked the Chief Steward, fascinated by the amazing imagination of the Reminnian Court.

"Certainly not to keep their people, who never give the rest of the world a nod, inside," said Tiberius.

"The ultimate back turn," Lisel commented, "a wall between themselves and the rest of the world."

"Their answer is a stone wall," Tiberius said.

"But they began the wall before we sent the message," the Chief Steward reasoned. "For some other reason they build a wall--ornamental perhaps?"

"More ornamental than protective," Tiberius agreed. "No battlements or towers, but as it begins to connect, I don't like the look of it."

"In what way?" the King inquired, on his feet to pace.

"A simple wall, higher than a garden wall, but lower than a fort. If it eventually stretches from the boulders of the Southeast to the Southwest, it effectively closes the border."

"Surely they will make a gate?" cried the Chief Steward.

"No gates yet," Tiberius said, "and I explored the extent of the thing myself."

"But not yet closed?" the King inquired again.

"Open many long stretches, but I don't expect to see gates."

"Maybe at the central road," the Chief Steward considered, as if he built such a wall himself.

Tiberius shrugged. "Reminnians make a gate connecting to our road? If they make a gate, I'll wager they put it miles off our road, for sheer perversity. Right now, I wouldn't wager on a gate anywhere."

"If they would meet with us, we could discuss it." The frustrated King paced the room.

"They won't." Tiberius felt certain.

"What do you propose we do?" the King asked.

"Nothing," said Tiberius.

The Chief Steward sank back with relief.

"This year," Tiberius continued. "Let them wall themselves in while we build our forces. Then, when they have one opening left, we ride through it and clean them out. They can't get behind us. We can supply to the wall while we force a steady stream to push them back into their precious sea. I don't need mountain horses for that; I need men, men, men. I will lose a fair number at the wall. I must have enough men to keep coming until they are destroyed, wall or no wall."

The Chief Steward gasped and clutched his heart.

"The wall also means they are contained while they are resettled," Tiberius finished with a grim, satisfied smile.

The King paced and considered. "Why? Why do we care?"

"Because they insult us," said Tiberius. "With their backs, with their wall, with their refusal to answer your message."

"Nothing changes." The King sighed.

Lisel excused herself. Nothing had changed. They argued about Reminnia again, but it put Tiberius off the horses. That allowed her time to plan and her mind worked best when her hands were busy.

In a quiet storeroom, adjacent to her own chamber, Lisel spread the fleece on the clean swept floor. Because Danny kept the sheep and their pens and fields as clean as possible, skirting for dirty clumps, bits of twigs and dried manure, went quickly. Her eager fingers sorted the wool, turning her hands soft and slippery with wool wax.

On the first truly hot day of summer, she washed and sun dried the fleece. Now light and lovely, the wool seemed to beg to be carded and spun as she carried it from the roof, where it had dried, to her chamber. Within the week, Lisel began the process. She opened her windows and door to the view of the Mountain, and settled with the carding combs. The fine wool felt like silk in her fingers. As she worked the fibers, she decided the crimp would lend itself best to weaving, rather than knitting, which pleased her. She imagined quiet hours at the loom, which always seemed to sooth her

When she began, at last, to spin, she discovered the yarn could be spun thin and remain strong or thick and remain soft. She settled on a rather fine grade for weaving.

On long summer evenings, after her day's chores, Lisel sat on the cool, north side of the castle, one eye on the mountains, a foot to her spinning wheel, with the wool slipping through her fingers, filling the spindle. Peace came over her that would carry her into the dark of the night. She would fall asleep, still feeling the fibers slipping through her fingers. By the time she finished spinning, Lisel trusted she would know what to weave with this yarn and what to do next about the Mountain.

The Chief Steward paid Lisel a call one evening. She had finished spinning for the day and sat with a cup of wine, resting near her doorway.

"We once walked the castle wall these mild summer evenings," he greeted her. "Would you care to walk it with me, tonight?"

"Thank you, no," she said. "I can see all I care to see of the world from here, but join me for a cup of wine, if you like."

He looked for a seat and discovered a sheepskin.

"We lost her lambing." Lisel fondly ran her hands over the wool. "Maybe next winter I'll make a vest."

"Enough for a coat," the Chief Steward said, "the way you're wasting away."

"Wasting away?" Lisel objected, pouring his

wine. "I'm stronger than I've been in years. I sheared seven mountain sheep, including a ram, myself." To his look of shock, she added honestly, "though it took two men to hold them."

The Chief Steward smiled, pleased to find her more fit than he expected. "Perhaps we waste away without you."

"What's on your mind, old man?" she asked.

He hesitated, uncertain whether to burden her with his problems.

"Come, my mind has enough ease for your woes tonight."

"Reminnia," he confessed.

"Ah," not her favorite topic but she would listen, for old time's sake.

"This thing Tiberius wants to do is wrong. We have no quarrel with them. They have not harmed us, other than our pride, which costs nothing but a little chagrin in our own eyes."

"What can I do about Reminnia?" she asked. *I cannot even see to the affairs of my own world.* She glanced to the mountains.

"Reason with the King," the Chief Steward begged. "He has heard me plead for Reminnia for so many years he turns a deaf ear."

So do I, Lisel thought.

"It's simply because Tiberius has nothing better to do," the Chief Steward complained. "He must stop building this army we no longer need and work for peace. More men must be sent back to the provinces.

Even feeding and outfitting so many troops breaks the backs of the few good men he leaves to the provinces. Women work in the fields."

"The King has not agreed to attack Reminnia," Lisel reminded him.

"The King lets him take the men, and now..."

"Yes, the wall insults him." Lisel admitted she felt the change in the King's mood, leaning more toward war.

"What the wall means we cannot possibly understand," the Chief Steward pleaded. "Reminnians do not see things in terms of wars. They only arm to defend their borders. They had attacks when we had our troubles in the southern provinces--but never, never have they attacked us."

"They don't need to," Lisel said. "They're rich. They take ships to lands beyond the sea. They bring exotic goods and food, all for themselves."

The Chief Steward could not deny that, nor could he honestly say he did not want some of those fine things, "but to take them by force is wrong. We must learn to trade."

"Trade didn't work out well for the Mountain King," Lisel reminded him.

"Lisel, you have grown bitter where once you were wise."

"I have grown bitter where once I was naive," she returned. "I am not pleased by my part in luring the Mountain King down to his death."

"No one could fault you for that accident."

"You believe that?" Lisel asked him. "You believe his death to be an accident?"

"Yes," said the Chief Steward. "I don't believe Tiberius always tells the truth, but that--to believe he sent a man to kill the Mountain King--does not make sense. He did not have to take such risk, not even to get a horse, and he didn't get a horse. Probably he has less chance of one now. Without the Mountain King no one will find anything in those mountains."

"Even if he did not send Jurgius to do it, he promoted the man who made a poor report about the matter."

"Sometimes," the Chief Steward said with a sigh, "the most convincing reports are the most false. I have come to believe that the truth often has more holes than well planned lies, where all the questions are anticipated and worked out ahead of time."

Lisel at least felt convinced that the Chief Steward had honestly struggled with the evidence and did not quickly or easily come to this conclusion. Her own intuitions in the matter, however, did not alter.

"I do not see how I can help you," she said.

"The King hesitates. If you speak against attack, he will make up his mind, for the right."

"The King no longer calls," Lisel said.

"He would," pressed the Chief Steward, "he would in a minute if he knew you were available to him." His keen eye told her she had only to give him the word to take straight to the King.

Lisel did not feel available to the King. "He turns

to his Wife now."

The Chief Steward shook his head. "Not for several weeks. She is with child, you know."

"With child?"

The Chief Steward nodded. "Not yet announced because he is not exactly pleased."

"He could foster again," Lisel said.

"Not the child of his Wife; too many people know in spite of no announcement."

"How far removed I am from the affairs of Court," Lisel observed, *and how little I care*, she added privately.

"We need you, Lisel," the Chief Steward begged, "When will you return to us?"

Lisel looked at the mountains and thought about leaving, not returning.

"A year has passed," the Chief Steward reminded her. "Grief lasting longer than a year is unhealthy. I've heard you say so yourself."

"I am no longer grieving," Lisel said with a clarity she discovered as she spoke, "but the affairs of this court no longer interest me."

The Chief Steward sat stunned. "What will you do, Lisel?"

"Spin and weave until I find other worthy work."

"Then you will do nothing to stop the destruction, this madness against Reminnia?"

"The Reminnian Court interests me less than this one," she said coldly. At that moment she understood how kings and queens made harsh decisions. She would sacrifice Reminnia and any number of Tiberius' unfortunate soldiers at that wall, to keep them off the Mountain.

The Chief Steward departed--a wounded man.

Actually, not quite a year had passed since the death of the Mountain King. A year perhaps, since his arrival, but his death coincided with Grand Parade, and though Lisel felt her time of mourning easing, she had not quite finished. The waves of paralyzing grief came less frequently, the nightmarish visions ceased, but her anger at the destruction of the Mountain King, and his absence, forever removed from her life, remained strong.

When Danny and the sheep moved south for the summer, Lisel sought another task to take her out of the castle as often as possible. She found it naturally, in another important interest: herbs, healing and medicine. Over the winter of her mourning, others tried not to bother her unnecessarily, but she had attended the usual burns, injuries and illness. Her supply of medicines, carefully extracted from herbs, must be replenished if life in this world insisted on going forward in spite the loss of the Mountain King.

Outside the castle wall Lisel and the castle cooks kept a substantial herb garden. They used some of the same herbs for cooking as Lisel used for healing preparations. She came late to garden that season, but the cooks had taken up her slack. She could see a back, bent and bobbing, as one cultivated and weeded through the garden rows. When she entered the garden gate, he straightened and waved a hand in greeting, but returned to hoeing, as if she might be a rare and fragile bird easily frightened away.

Lisel moved through the garden, murmuring greetings to her plants that she appeared to have abandoned that spring. The basil stood well up, welcoming her return, and dill planted that season also rose strong and fine. The blooming Chamomile begged to be clipped. The cooks had contained it from threatening to take over the end of the garden, but left unclipped what they called her "weed." Though Lisel intended only to make a look-see visit to the garden that morning, she could not resist clipping the eager white and yellow flowers. The Lemon Balm and Lavender plants, also primarily her domain, nodded as if in relief to feel Lisel's hand checking their stalks and leaves. She and the cook met at the Thyme bed. He finished cultivating the soil, and pointed out, as though she not been absent for the first planting and tending of the season, how well it looked. He drew his shears from his tool belt and snipped a few branches; some for himself to take back to the kitchen, and some for her.

Lisel thanked him and waved good bye as he shook the cricks from his back and left the garden. As for herself, she sat on a garden bench in the early spring sun, and closed her eyes. The sun rose higher, toward mid-day, and drew out the scents of the garden. Lisel rested and let them heal her, as truly as if she drank their substance in a brew. She dozed and woke with a jolt, when a bee buzzed her ear the way unwelcome thoughts could sting without warning. The Chamomile flowers were wilting in the hot sun. Lisel rose and made her way home with the bouquet She'd be back; she had good work and old friends here, too.

Work in the cultivated garden reminded Lisel that she also needed to restock supplies growing wild. She got out her baskets and the collection of bags in all sizes she used to collect, and keep her herbs separated, on foraging trips. These bags, some made by her mother, some by herself, had needle work labels indicating which plants went in each one. Her mother thought, and Lisel agreed, as she smoothed folded the bags into her basket, that stitching a facsimile of the plant in small stitches on the bag helped fix in one's mind its details. While stitching, as a young girl, around the pattern of the leaf, or the flower, drawn by her mother she learned to distinguish one from the other when gathering in the wild.

The wild Valerian seemed to call to her from the meadows. If she were to have more of this root for Valerian wine, she must go soon to the area where the best plants grew and clip some flower heads, forcing the roots to grow stronger.

The Valerian grove she liked best, at the edge of the meadow, looked the same as last year at this time, though to Lisel the rest of the world seemed painfully changed. As she clipped off the clusters of pink and white flowers, she murmured apologies to the plants. She would not clip them all, only those from which she intended to harvest later. Did the plants understand? She sat on the meadow wall, and remembered walking there with the Mountain King while Rufus danced in the dandelions. He crowned her his Queen not far from this place. Now, she looked down at her hands, with the shears dangling from them, and felt as savaged as the shorn Valerian plants. Would she grow a stronger root by having her flowers shorn? She did not feel confident; more than her flowers had been clipped. He was her root and they had torn her from him. She did not feel certain that healing strength could grow from that wound. Rising from the wall, she forced herself to walk further, to see the mint that grew profusely along the brook bank. She refused, on this glorious morning, to think dark thoughts.

The King observed Lisel's increased activity and saw her recovering in all aspects except her relationship with him. "You make a great many foraging trips," he commented as she passed him with her baskets one morning.

"If you stock for war," she replied, "I must stock for injuries and wounds."

"True," he agreed. Though relieved she seemed

to take interest in the affairs of the Court after the chilling comment reported to him by the Chief Steward, he did not feel content with their relationship. He blocked her way, causing her to linger with him.

"And your Wife is with child," she said with a smile. "I will collect special herbs to make the birth easier for her."

"And what will you do," he asked, longing to touch her, "to make that birth easier for me?"

She traced a finger down his worried cheek. "Come to hold your hand the night it is born," she promised, "to keep you out from underfoot of the midwives."

"I will look forward to that," he said catching her hand.

Her hand slipped through his to hurry on her way. He felt farewell, rather than hello, in her touch.

The idea occurred to Lisel, while she gathered leaves for Blackberry tea, near the place the road turned up the Mountain, that she could go up the Mountain by herself. At first she could figure no way to arrange an exploratory journey without riling the King who wanted nothing said about the Mountain. He now used the excuse that it upset his Wife, who was with child.

Pricked by the thorns on the Blackberry vine, her finger spurted blood. She stared at the red trickle for a moment and recalled her blood joined with the blood of the Mountain King. She would do this thing.

The trip would take more than a day, but she had spent several days and nights out of the castle while lambing. She needed only a destination they would not question, to make a trek up the Mountain. The idea charged her with such excitement she could scarcely think of anything else. The midsummer weather would be warm enough to sleep outside. They camped last year, even earlier in the spring. Once there, Silas and Hannah would welcome her.

Maybe, she hesitated, *they will not welcome me*. Perhaps they saw her connected to the plot to deceive the Mountain King. *All the more reason*, she resolved. She must go to them, tell them and take counsel with them about the Mountain.

To disappear without warning would arouse a search; she did not care to risk that. She mentioned to the Chief Steward that she wanted to take a horse and travel a few days journey into the Northwest Province. She knew places where particularly fine herbs once grew, and would like to see if the plants still produced.

"And a couple of people to help you?" he asked.

"I can see to myself," she declined.

"But to make campsites, and all, you need help."

"Don't intend to camp," she laughed as if the idea never occurred to her. "I know many people way in Northwest Provinces with whom I could stop over. Extra people with me would be an imposition."

"How long will you gone?" he asked, worrying before she even started her journey.

"A few days, maybe a week, depending on what I find," she said. *Maybe the rest of my life*, she thought.

She packed lightly. She dared not look as if she packed for the rest of her life and doing so, realized how little her possessions meant to her. She decided to take the sheepskin with her, for a saddle blanket; no one would question that, or her herb baskets and bags. Over the yarn skeins from the flop eared sheep, she debated. She had finished spinning, though she put off weaving until next winter when she would need the project on dark cold days. She quickly rolled them inside a few changes of clothing and tucked them in her herb bags. The baskets held plenty of provisions. Though she said she would visit cottages along the way, she would not be expected to go empty handed into a provincial home.

On the morning she set out, the grooms in the stable selected a trim sorrel horse and saddled it with the sheepskin. They wished her well on her herb gathering journey. No one, except the King's Wife, ever wished Lisel other than well, not even Tiberius.

She set out toward the Northwest Province and passed the crossroad to the mountain road without turning onto it. First, she made a side trip to the camp once kept by the Mountain King when he came to visit. The thought occurred to her that if Silas came down the Mountain with a message for her, he might go to that campsite. She wished she'd thought of checking earlier, or leaving a message there for him. At the camp, she found the site undisturbed. It did not appear to have been used by Silas. The place did not feel the same as last summer when she made love to the Mountain King. She found no trace of his presence among the rocks and bushes. Suddenly, eager to be about her adventure, she turned and trotted down the trail, and across the hills, to pick up the Mountain road at a place far from the crossroads.

In her youth, she made may secret missions among the rolling hills of the high plains, but never felt so alone as in these years of her midlife. Once she ran messages and supplies from her father's home base in the Northeast Province to the band of three, the King, Tiberius and the Chief Steward, in their hideouts. Those days she moved between friends. Now, she had only herself to rely upon, and no certain welcome at the end of her journey. Nevertheless, she felt as sure as when a young girl on dangerous missions. Her bravery, though tempered by knowledge of danger, felt sharpened by the wisdom of maturity. She had little to lose; her life in the castle mattered little to her now. By the time she could see it below, it looked as small as a toy. She wondered how it ever absorbed so much of her interest and her life. The Mountain drew her upward. She did not press the sorrel horse. She recalled how the previous journey winded the horses and took frequent breaks. At times she dismounted to walk or sit in the shade, when the curve in the road turned away from the sun. When she found springs bubbling out of the mountainside, she let the horse drink. Come night, she would sleep on the sheepskin, camped in the road as on her first journey up the Mountain. The next day she would proceed. She expected, in spite of rest stops, to make better time than last year because she did not require the long breaks the Chief Steward needed, and did not trail loaded pack horses. She felt light and free, traveling steadily up the Mountain. The only thing that would have increased her pleasure would be anticipating the Mountain King to greet her at the gate.

He would laugh away her tears. "Pushed me over the cliff did they? Oh sure." He would take her in his arms, and hold her, and that would be the end of her grief. She would never leave him. She would tell him how her winter of grief brought her quickly "to the point in life where I need the ease of not so many tasks to beckon when I rise each morning." Her grief struck her down and raised her up; aged her and restored her youthful fervor.

She traveled as far as safe in the evening shadows but had wisely picked a night of full moon to commence this journey. She needed no campfire; she simply spread the sheepskin on the ground and reclined against the mountain wall, as she once reclined with the Mountain King. Ah, if only Silas would appear to tell her he had been watching her up the road. In the lonely purple moment daylight vanished, she did not tease herself with visions of the Mountain King, but she did long for Silas.

She had not rested long before she heard another

solitary horse on the road. *Silas*? She listened. Her horse stirred, sensing another horse. Not Silas, she determined; he would come from the upward direction. This step came, as her horse turned now to watch, from behind.

She listened intently, her heart beating harder than she preferred. Only one--might be Silas, coming from a hidden trail, on the gray gelding. She rose.

The approaching horse stopped, as if the unseen rider heard her move. Though she longed to ease the tension by calling out for Silas, she did not. She had no intention to reveal his name, or that she hoped to meet anyone in this place. Did the rider know she waited around the next curve, or did this person decide, coincidentally, to stop for the night so close?

Lisel discarded coincidence; too many coincidences already happened on this road. Whoever waited around the curve knew she was here and did not proceed. She had no weapons, other than clipping shears for herbs. She had endurance. She could wait quietly as long as necessary to see who lurked in the curve behind her. After awhile, she saw a flicker of a light. Her silent companion had lighted a lantern. That did not draw her either. Whoever, must be a less intrepid camper than she, who lighted no fire or lantern.

After what seemed a long time, long enough for her heart to quit beating out of control, she heard footsteps on the road. She stiill hoped against the odds for Silas, but was not surprised to see Jurgius.

The sorrel horse blinked and stamped at the glaring lantern. Lisel shielded her eyes from the sudden intense light.

"Looking for lost dogs, Lisel?" Jurgius asked.

"Didn't have to look far. I sat still and one found me."

"What are you doing here?"

She could say, *gathering herbs what grows in the* Instead, she countered him. "What are you doing here?"

"Following you."

"To give a report of my journey? To whom?"

"The King ordered no one to come up the mountains."

"I'm sure he didn't mean me," Lisel dismissed him. "I go where I please--always have, always will."

Jurgius stood in the road, with the lantern, looking very stupid, very annoyed, and only slightly dangerous.

"I am sure," she shook her finger, "he meant Tiberius and you, too."

"I was not told of any exceptions and it's my job to..." he faltered.

"Your job to what?"

"Prevent anyone from going up."

"You haven't prevented, only followed. Why didn't you catch up earlier and force me back?"

"I thought you would turn back."

"Why?"

"I don't know," he admitted with irritation. "I

don't even know why you're here."

"Yes, you do. You said it."

"Looking for a lost dog?" he repeated.

"And a lost horse, and a lost King," she finished.

"Dangerous," he warned her.

"Not until you arrived."

Jurgius in that moment could almost be mistaken for well meaning as he pleaded with her. "You are a good woman, Lisel. Why do you torment yourself by not accepting the accident?"

"You must be hungry, Jurgius," Lisel replied, "and I doubt you brought provisions if you didn't think you'd be staying the night." She offered him the bread and sausage so quickly; he drew back as if she drew a weapon on him.

"My but you're nervous! Careful you don't tumble over the edge."

He accepted the food, without thanks, and ate.

"Put out the lantern," she ordered.

"Why?"

"There's a full moon. We don't need it."

He put out the lantern, but walked up and down the small stretch of road before her, as if he did not know what to do next until she ordered him.

"Have you groomed your horse?"

"What's it to you?"

"You caught up in a hurry. If you had followed my pace all day, I would have heard you earlier. Tend the horse so it doesn't get chilled. We're not going further until day light."

"We're not going further at daylight," Jurgius announced. "We're going back."

"Speak for yourself. I'm well supplied and traveling on."

"We'll see about that in the morning," he said as he went to tend his horse. He chose to move his horse close to hers, and settled himself down uncomfortably close to her. "Keeping you in sight."

"To make a good report?" She moved away, shook out her sheepskin and rearranged herself. "You can see me from here, if you don't fall asleep, but I'll smell less of you."

Jurgius, she observed, not only slept on his watch, he snored and rolled about. She hoped he would roll off the cliff. If so, she intended to claim she threw him over. Who would believe he rolled over in his sleep--too good to be true.

It occurred to her, watching him sleep, she could kill him with the clipping shears and roll him over the edge. Even if he woke and dragged her over with him, he would die.

She felt disinclined to lower herself to murder. Better to let him wake in the morning and find her gone, if he did not wake early.

Jurgius woke suddenly the next morning, at the sound of her moving about to saddle her horse. No denying he slept, but he leaped to his feet with instant recovery. Probably, she decided, she couldn't have killed him and was glad she had not tried. A glorious day to continue her journey, in spite of him.

"Where are you going?"

"Same destination as yesterday," she replied, mounting. She preferred to eat as she traveled, rather than waste time with him in a camp, or share more food with him.

"Lisel, stop." He grabbed her horse's halter.

"Don't," she snapped. "You don't need more accidents to report."

"Please," he begged, "come back with me."

"I want to see the place where the road gave way, a place big enough to take a man and a horse."

"Dangerous," he insisted.

"If you worry for my safety, come with me. Show me the place."

Jurgius considered.

"I want to look down and see what's left of his body and finish my year of mourning."

"Not a pretty sight," Jurgius said, "after a winter."

"A long ways down," she reminded him, "only a glimpse."

"Maybe nothing left, if the wild animals got to them."

"Them?" she asked.

"The man and the horse," he said quickly.

"Then I will be satisfied with the break in the road, but I must see something to convince me such an accident happened."

"Unreasonable," Jurgius muttered, but he agreed.

"You go first," she said. "I'll follow, since it's so

dangerous."

He looked displeased. "I'd like to have a bite to eat."

"Can't you eat and ride at the same time as I do?" She did not offer him more food.

He carried emergency rations in his saddle pack and found them. Irritated, he mounted and rode ahead. She followed without letting him out of sight. She did not intend to be surprised inside a curve and he dared not appear afraid she would harm him from the rear.

A couple of hours into the morning they found the road blocked with boulders.

"What now?" she asked.

"Turn back," Jurgius suggested.

"Can't you move them?"

He stared at her in disbelief. "Not by myself, and even as strong as you are Lisel, not with your help." He dismounted to survey the obstruction. "A rock slide. More could come down behind them. A rock slide could kill a person on this road," he mused as if noting another hypothetical way a person might die on the mountain. "We should turn back."

Lisel laughed. "Those boulders have been there awhile. See how the weeds grow around them?" Looking up she saw a high mountain shelf above, but no loose rocks poised to crush them. She had the distinct impression, whether he saw it or not, those boulders had been rolled off to block the road.

"We could leave the horses here and climb over,"

Lisel suggested. "I see a foot hold."

"Climb over? Leave the horses? Are you crazy?"

"I am a woman on a mission of love and my energy is not yet spent," she declared.

"If one rockslide happened here, likely to be more ahead," Jurgius aargued. "No one can pass until the rocks are cleared."

Lisel let tears slip down her cheeks. She found it easy after all those she shed this past year, and knew them to be fatal with some men. "Please, Jurgius, climb over and see how the road looks."

If the rock pile slipped, she would watch closely to make a full report, how he died.

"Craziness!"

"Please," she begged. "If you tell me the road is impassable on the other side, I will accept your word and go home."

"Alright." He put a foot to the first step up in the rock and pulled himself up.

"See? It's not so hard," she encouraged him. "I climbed rocks like that as a child."

Jurgius grunted, but went up and over, out of sight.

Quickly, Lisel turned her horse and grabbed the lead rein on his horse. She pulled it around, facing down hill.

"The road right here," he called from the other side of the pile, "is not so bad." He sounded disappointed. She expected him to lie and declare it impossible.

"Go a little further. See if there's another slide," she pleaded. "If it's clear, I'll tie the horses and join you."

"A bad idea," he called but his voice trailed off indicating he moved up the road.

Maybe he plotted to get her on the rocks and push her over, but Lisel had her own plan, though not quite as ambitious. She snapped the rein on the rump of his horse. The startled animal snorted and flew the only possible direction, down the road.

"What's that?" Jurgius called, hearing the horse.

"Your horse slipped over the cliff." She bent forward, urging her horse to trot fast as she dared around the curve, down the Mountain.

He might have been standing on top of the boulders, as she disappeared, but she didn't turn back when he hollered after her. "Stop! Come back!"

She trotted around curves, glad for the light little sorrel. She heard Jurgius running behind her but he'd never catch her without a horse.

"Where's my horse?" she last heard him bellow.

His horse, Lisel found not far down the road. It had paused after finding no alarm worth the effort and tugged at a tuft of grass growing near the edge of the road. She caught the lead rein and jerked it along behind, as she continued down hill. She wouldn't have to keep a fast pace for long. As soon as the exhilaration wore off, she slowed and tied the lead rein of Jurgius' horse behind her own saddle.

He could bellow and bash his head on the rocks

all morning, but he'd never catch up with his horse. She noted she had his water jug and precious lantern, too. Down proved easier than up, and even with two hours lost going forward that morning, she expected to reach the castle by nightfall. Jurgius would take longer.

She hoped whoever rolled those boulders down on the road watched from above and saw her strand him there. She hoped they rolled more boulders down on him. She imagined buzzards swooping at him, dead or alive, pecking out his lying eyes.

By early evening, still long with summer light, she stopped to rest the horses so they would not arrive hot and exhausted. While resting she realized that she had gathered no herbs. Empty baskets would look odd. On every foraging journey she came home with something. Much too late in the day for collecting leaves or flower heads and she did not like taking from the life giving plants only to discard their offerings later. What to do? The willow trees at the edge of the brook, where the horses drank, beckoned slightly in the breeze. A few of their branches, cut for stripping the bark, would fill the baskets. She had not brought a knife suitable for cutting branches, but by opening her shears wide to the blade, she made the necessary cuts. The willow branches poking out of her baskets did indeed make the baskets appear to overflow.

At sundown Lisel rode through the gate, calm and collected, with the willow branches gently swishing. Jurgius' horse, on a lead rein, trotted behind the sorrel.

The grooms rushed out to greet her and before they asked, she explained, "I found this horse on the road." She appeared to care more that her baskets be handed down gently than for their alarm that the horse was the one Jurgius took, two days and a night ago.

The second in command, a senior officer, arrived running as Lisel mounted the castle steps, "Where...

"Where?" she repeated. "I've been gathering willow branches, for the bark. I'll soak the rest for weaving baskets."

"The horse--where did you find the horse?"

"On the road, not far away. Is there some concern?"

"Not yet."

The Senior Officer weighed his responsibilities. The Fort Commander's horse was found wandering on the road, and he gone two days. Jurgius, same as Tiberius, never told where he went or when to expect him back. Tiberius did so to keep his men on the alert for him, anytime, anywhere. Jurgius, the annoyed Senior Officer surmised, had delusions of being Tiberius. No other Fort Commander he served under behaved so high handed. Now he must make decisions.

He sent a scouting party that night, with torches, to search the area in case Jurgius had been thrown and injured. No luck, and no sight of Jurgius by morning. He felt compelled to report the accident to higher authority--the King or Tiberius.

Asking to speak to the King he felt out of his reach. Tiberius often spent this part of the summer in the low plains training troops. If he was not there, other Fort Commanders would be there. The senior among them could be reported to about the missing person. Tiberius did not respect hesitation in the face of crisis in officers. He'd rather help a decisive man out of a bad decision than an indecisive coward lace a boot. The second scouting party returned mid-day with no clue about Jurgius. A runner left for the low plains within the hour.

Before the message reached Tiberius, but too far gone to call back, Jurgius walked through the castle gates under cover of dark the next night. He gave no explanations and abused the Senior Officer for sending word to Tiberius on such slight provocation.

Lisel sat in the shade by her door, peeling long strips of curling bark from the willow branches with a small sharp knife. She told the Chief Steward she did not stay away long because she found excellent willow, closer than she expected. She chatted with more animation than usual.

He felt relieved at her return. He did not like her to travel alone, though the sun on her face brought out a light peppering of freckles, reminding him of her youth. Her smile, as she stripped the bark in delicate curls, and the sound of pleasure in her voice, though he cared little for the fine points of bark teas and basket weaving, warmed him.

Surveying the Mountain, Lisel felt resolved about a few matters, if not all her concerns. While she had wanted to go all the way up to Silas and Hannah, she felt relieved to know the people were not helpless. They had blocked the road and, though a party of soldiers could move the boulders, it would be difficult. In the meantime, a little more precious time, she need not worry about unwelcome traffic up the mountain road. Furthermore, if she had been observed coming up the Mountain, whoever watched would also have seen Jurgius. That would have discouraged contact with her, but her treatment of him would also have been observed. As much as she enjoyed her prank, and as useless and childish as it felt in the larger picture, she realized it carried the message she wanted to send the mountain people.

When Jurgius returned she felt slightly disappointed they had not pushed boulders over on him, nor had he been attacked by wild animals nor died of thirst and exposure. She paid him no mind and he did not look for her.

Tiberius found Lisel a few days later. He leaned through the window where she worked, grinding dried herbs into powder to replenish her medicinal crocks. "So, I am not the only horse thief in this Court."

Lisel gave him only a cursory glance. "You? You

have no reputation as a horse thief."

Tiberius laughed. "True. Your skill exceeds mine, Lisel. Next time I want to steal a horse, I'll send you."

"You might have done better to send me the last time. But, I did not steal a horse. I found one on the road and brought it home. Have I been accused of stealing it?"

"And worse," he said, looking amused. "I am pleased to find you so fit and as clever as always."

Lisel dismissed him with a shrug, but he reached through the window to turn her face to his with a finger beneath her chin. "It's the most amusing event in this castle for a long time."

"We are short on amusements," she agreed, jerking away from his touch.

"Even more amusing than the sight of the King's Wife looking at her belly, wondering what happened." Tiberius laughed again and went on his way.

Lisel smiled to herself; that she had embarrassed Jurgius before his Commander in Chief and the King, who would hear the story from Tiberius, amused her, too.

Turning back to her work, and her own thoughts she made peace with herself. Though the road remained closed to her, it remained closed to others, as well. In the meantime, she would follow the Mountain King's request by remaining in this Court to watch for his interests. Though they had never been close, his daughter, now with child, would be one of his concerns. The poor girl might not know what happened to her, or what to expect in childbirth. Lisel sighed and doubted whether the King's Wife would pay attention to her advice.

On Grand Parade banquet day Lisel announced her mourning completed, but withdrew from the celebration as soon as decently acceptable. She planned to begin a new year by starting her weaving. The small loom in her chamber had not been used for some time; the larger one in the workroom where the Court met usually proved more convenient.

For this work she wanted solitude and privacy. The small loom was much like one she had as a girl. Though that one was destroyed, when her provincial cottage burned in a battle, the Chief Steward had one like it built for her when she came to the castle. His gift had deeply pleased her. Now she threaded it with the light silky thread from the flop-eared ewe. She had spun it quite fine, and found herself amazed and thrilled how strong and how smooth the texture. She marveled how easy the wool proved in her fingers. She had not dyed it; the washed ivory seemed an excellent color for a shawl to display to advantage on her dark dresses. Lisel usually preferred not to call attention to herself, but this piece of work she wanted everyone to notice. She wanted to announce, "this shawl, like no other shawl, is made of the love of the

Mountain King."

The shawl would not be large, but she intended to leave a long delicate fringe. She planned to work slowly, stretching the pleasure of the work into the fall days ahead. Then, on the dreariest day of winter, she would bloom in the beautiful ivory shawl.

Lisel wove on days her thoughts turned to the Mountain King. This year, though she didn't believe it possible, she discovered her thoughts were not all dark. She could remember their exchanged visits, and treasure those memories without always crashing into the abyss of his death. Those days she wove. If her thoughts turned dark, she moved to other tasks.

While Lisel wove, the King's Wife progressed in her pregnancy. She knew how the baby got there, but felt more frightened how it would get out. The midwives alternately reassured her and terrified her. The King did not come to her as he did the previous winter. The midwives explained he did not, because it would not be good for the baby. Beyond that, the King felt uneasy at the sight of her growing belly. The bigger she grew, the more he avoided her. She blamed the baby for his rejection. Among castle service women who did not keep babies, a pregnant King's Wife who would keep her baby, caused more resentment than her bad temper already incurred. The girl grew more and more unhappy as her pregnancy progressed

The Chief Steward made an official announcement. When rumors must be verified, he sent word throughout the provinces: the King's Wife expected a baby who would be the King's heir. The King proceeded with grim determination. He had undertaken this matter and did not retreat; though he felt he needed an heir about as much as he needed a Wife.

The Chief Steward, to reassure him, told him he might feel differently by the time the heir grew up. After all, none of them were getting any younger. Somehow that did not improve the King's spirits. The Chief Steward amused himself with the plans for the heir's arrival: the announcements, the supplies, and cogitating whether the baby would be a girl or a boy.

The King cared not a whit whether a girl or a boy; the Child would be his heir. He announced it and would live with it. He remembered Lisel saying she would come to him on the night the baby arrived and interpreted that meant she would mark the end of her removal from him. With that prospect, he anticipated the birth of the baby. By early spring he would have an heir, but he would also have Lisel again.

By mid winter, Lisel finished waving her shawl. This shawl, unlike the heavier ones she wrapped herself in against the cold, was a single layer. If draped across her arms, it swept low in back with fringe almost touching the hem of her skirt. She could wind it around her head and her neck, framing her face in a cloud of white with fringe flowing over her shoulders and down her back. She found it soft enough to wear under another shawl without the slightest bulky discomfort. She could tie it around her bodice and make any dress fit for a banquet. Its softness, unmatched by any other garment, she loved next to her skin. She could press her face the soft fabric and feel the love of the Mountain King caressing her cheek. Sometimes, in private, by the light of a candle before her looking glass, she draped the shawl over and around her nude body, letting it fall slightly to reveal her breasts. The fringe played out over her pubic hair, another layer of soft fluff. In such a shawl she would have made love to him. She studied her body, adorned in the creamy wool of his love, and knew he would have found her beautiful even if she lived to be a wrinkled old crone. In this shawl she felt eternally young and beautiful.

Lisel decided the first person to see the completed shawl should be Danny. She wrapped it around her shoulders, under heavier wraps, and made the first journey of winter to visit him.

"Did you think I forgot you?" she greeted him.

"I think you moved past needing to wrestle with sheep," Danny replied. He smiled, pleased to see her.

"I have been weaving," she said, cheeks bright with excitement and rosy from the winter cold. "Look."

Danny at first refused to touch the beautiful shawl for fear his weather worn fingers would snag it.

Lisel insisted. "Just wool we sheared together

101

and quite strong."

Danny's eyes lighted as he touched the fine stuff.

They walked out to field to look at the lop-eared ewe, but she had no interest in Lisel this year. As they walked toward the shack for a sip of hot broth, she asked, "did you and your nephew travel the provinces to shear the dowry sheep?"

"No," said Danny, "we did the Eastern Provinces, North and South. Southeast drove theirs up to us."

"And did your nephew do well with them?"

"He did." Danny said.

"How grew the wool?"

"Good," Danny said.

Lisel noticed his taciturn manner. "How is your nephew?"

"Fine." He did not sound fine. After a time, as they sat together, Danny confessed, "I worry for him."

"What's the matter?"

"He says he'd rather die himself than kill."

Or be killed, Lisel thought. "You don't think he'll harm himself?"

"Oh no," Danny answered quickly. "He knows that's a crime--destruction of the King's property."

"Oh, Danny, I would like to assure you I could arrange for him not to be taken, but I have little influence at court now. I have removed myself so much from their affairs."

"Please don't," Danny protested. "He would be distressed to be brought to the Court's attention, in any way."

Lisel walked back to the castle that afternoon with a weight on her mind. She wanted to ask the Chief Steward to see that one young man from the Northeast Province be returned as a sheepherder, but recalled how bitterly she refused his request to intervene with the King regarding Reminnia. Nevertheless, she must try, for Danny.

The Chief Steward's door stood ajar, where he worked into the evening on his books and calculations. Tiberius planning for war meant the Chief Steward planned for supplies.

Lisel tapped lightly and peeked inside.

The old man's rose from his worktable to greet her with both hands extended. "Lisel!" His hands clasped hers. Discerning their chill, he briskly rubbed them between his own, though they were not much warmer. "Cold hands, but your cheeks look rosy. From a long walk?"

"Out to visit Danny," Lisel said. "After spending so much time there last winter, I neglected him this year."

"You've been busy," the Chief Steward dismissed her concern. "Weaving, and this lovely shawl is the result." He lifted a piece of fringe delicately on his long fingers.

"My labor of love," she announced.

The Chief Steward inspected all around and said with genuine care, "I am so relieved, Lisel, to hear you say a labor of love, not of grief. You do heal?"

"At least enough to notice the cares of others

again," she said. "I need to ask a favor of you, but recall how I dismissed your concerns a few months ago."

The Chief Steward pulled out a chair for her and poured a glass of wine. "Ask me, Lisel. I am so pleasured to have you call on me, to need me. If in my power, you know I will do it for you."

Lisel sighed. "Danny worries for his nephew, a sensitive lad, and good with animals. I know myself from working with him."

"And fears to be a soldier?" the Chief Steward guessed.

Lisel nodded.

The Chief Steward reached for his record book. He opened the pages and let his finger roam until he found the Northeast Province.

"Knowing the risk now, and how I did nothing to stop this war, I feel responsible."

The Chief Steward made a notation in his book. "I will try, Lisel, but can guarantee nothing. Tiberius gets first choice, and if the young man is fit..." he shrugged, "I can do nothing."

Lisel smiled, "but you will try; more hope than I offered you."

The Chief Steward poured his wine and sat back to sip it. "I have made my peace with this thing. It will happen, and neither your fault or mine."

"Your conscience is more clear than mine," she said.

"Why should it be on our consciences?" asked

the Chief Steward. "Why hasn't the Reminnian Court done a thing to help themselves? Why do they build that senseless wall, that outrages our King?"

"I have never understood Reminnian ways."

"I thought I did, once," sighed the Chief Steward, "but I give up. They turn their backs and refuse to see what is coming upon them. Perhaps some good will come of it, eventually."

"How?"

"To make the world one with borders open, the records and knowledge they own available to all..." The Chief Steward's agitation propelled him out of his chair. "I have asked, and asked, to see the records. History belongs to us all, not just to them. I have recorded only the years here, and what I remember. I want to clarify the records, but they will not share their knowledge."

"I have always called them selfish, but now it rings hollow. I was selfish myself this past year."

"You were grieving," the Chief Steward said.

"You forgive me for turning you away?"

"Forgive? You must forgive me for coming to you in such a time. How insensitive I must have been to consider it." He touched her shoulder and felt the shawl. "If this work is the measure of your love, it was deep and beautiful--the extent of which I did not fathom."

"Nor I, until too late."

"Last of the original three kings," the Chief Steward mused, "and perhaps he too died by his foibles, as he said the others did."

The Chief Steward felt their friendship restored as far as possible, though he recognized a change in Lisel. She would never be the same as before the Mountain King. Some things, once done, cannot be undone. She took her leave, her hand slipping gently through his. He contemplated the place where she sat, her unfinished wine in the cup, like her unfinished life. Some things, once done, maybe can be undone! He turned the pages in the census book to the Southeast Province. Not this year, but soon, a young man, Claudio, from the house of Kyle, would come of age. The Chief Steward vowed to put every measure of his wit into keeping that young man from Tiberius.

The heir arrived on a rainy afternoon too early to suit the midwives. The King, his hair literally on end from running his hands through it, called for Lisel. Though not enthused about an heir, the possibility it might die terrified him. A fleeting wish that the Mountain King would disappear, and the death happened. Now, though he confessed to no one how he wished he'd never got into this domestic arrangement, it too might take a dark turn. He did not wish harm to his Wife or an innocent infant and felt responsible, yet helpless, at their danger.

Lisel was surprised to hear the baby arrived early, but not surprised the King called for her. She did not realize his frantic state until at his chamber door.

"Goodness, you're more distressed than I expected."

"I thought babies got born in the night and took a long time." He threw up his hands to go tearing through his hair again. "This one arrived so fast, without warning! I feel we've been attacked, and found unready--the baby may not live."

"I have not heard that," Lisel said. "I heard only that the baby is born, and a boy."

"And very small, and...." he sat down, safe now in Lisel's presence, to hold his head.

Lisel touched his shoulder. "What worries you most?"

He sighed and confessed, "that harm should come to it, or to my Wife, and be my fault. I did not need a Wife or an heir, but they should not come to harm." He clutched her warm hand.

Lisel disengaged her hand. "Let's find out how they fare before worrying too much, or about the wrong things."

The King sighed again. Lisel taking charge revived him sufficiently to put his hair in order and present an almost normal appearance before she returned with one of the midwives who carried a small bundle.

"Here's your baby." Lisel said and took his hand. "Alive and tiny, requiring close attention, but breathing and wetting and doing all he can to please you."

The King peered into the bundle held by the midwife. All to be seen of the baby was a reddish face, with eyes clamped shut, and fingers so tiny they looked like a fine line drawing of a hand curled against its cheeks.

The King stared, "the hair?"

"That will go away," said the midwife. "It's because he came so early."

The baby's wild black hair, not settled on a hairline, wandered into its face and out again at random.

"You are sure?" asked the King.

"Oh yes," said the midwife, "may not even stay black."

"This baby does not look like my Wife, or me, does it?" The King felt unsure of everything facing this baby stranger.

Lisel laughed at the tiny hairy infant. "That's his mountain blood." She saw a surprising resemblance to the dark haired children who ran about underfoot at the palace of the Mountain King. She took the baby from the midwife for a closer look.

"The Mountain King did not have black hair."

"He had white hair, but we don't know what color hair he had as a baby, or a child," Lisel said, *or a young man,* she added to herself. The thought struck her with unexpected poignancy that she had not known him in his youth. She handed the baby back to the midwife.

"How is my Wife?" the King asked.

"A quick, easy birth for her, but for this one, too soon, such a cold day, and us not ready...."

"But all is well now," Lisel interrupted, lest the list of terrors upset the King again.

"She gave us a time," the midwife confessed, with an anxious glance to the King, "and did not want to see the baby."

"Why not?" asked the King. Although he found it ugly, he couldn't take his eyes off it.

"She wanted a girl, and when we told her a boy, she began screaming--worse than in her labor."

"Let her rest," Lisel soothed. "Do you want to hold the baby, before she takes him away?"

The King did not want to hold the baby though felt he must, after hearing of his Wife's rejection, lest it be rumored that he too rejected the baby. Such a tiny, weightless thing, the midwife placed in his hands, and wrapped so tightly, he could scarcely feel a body. He held it, and looked at the hairy face, with squeezed closed eyes that refused to acknowledge its birth had occurred. He almost relaxed, feeling competent, when it did not cry. He smiled. *How foolish to be upset by a mere baby.*

The baby slit open its eyes. They darted side to side, then closed, as if no more pleased to see this world than his parents were to see him.

The King handed the baby back to the midwife. After dismissing her, with the baby, the King sank down, feeling weak in the knees. "Are they all so ugly, Lisel?"

"He's early," Lisel reminded him. "Given another week or two, he would have filled out and smoothed the hair line. Other than that--he looks like a baby."

"Did yours look like that?" he asked.

"Ours," she emphasized, "were full term and bigger-- with lighter hair--that's about all I recall."

The King shook his head to dismiss such visions and looked on Lisel. He saw she wore the lovely white shawl.

"I thought I would make love to you tonight," he said sadly, "but I cannot."

Lisel did not feel disappointed. "A rather stressful afternoon. I really meant to be available to you but didn't hear until after the birth."

"Happened so quickly," he said dismissing that topic. He touched the fringe on her shawl. His fingers lingered but did not touch her arm. "I see you are no longer mine. You belong to another."

Perhaps it was thoughtless to wear the shawl to come to him, but she had not planned it so. She wore it often and this was not the first time he had seen it. She did not apologize.

"He is dead but you wear this shawl like wedding garments. To touch you would be as callous as taking another man's wife."

Not, thought Lisel, *if the wife offered herself*, but she did not offer. She felt secure and serene in the protection of the Mountain King's shawl; a mantle of his love spread over her.

"If he were not dead," said the King, "perhaps

you could have loved both of us. Now, I can see, I would somehow violate you."

Lisel observed his insight brought him no comfort. She pitied him but did not relent and make love to him.

"There are other ways to be together," she suggested. "You had a difficult afternoon; let me massage your back."

Gratefully, he allowed her to pull off his shirt. He leaned forward, resting his head on his table, while she poured oil into her hands, to warm it. When she smoothed it onto his skin, he thought how he had missed her. How hard the knots tied without her hands to release them. How he wished closing his eyes would shut out the world the way the baby refused to acknowledge it.

Early expulsion of the baby from her body was first in a series of rejections of the infant by the King's Wife. Though recovering well from a quick birth, she refused to nurse the baby. No other woman in the castle had given birth recently enough to nurse. Concern rose for the tiny infant. The midwives asked the Chief Steward to send for a nursing mother from one of the Northern Provinces. Already, frail, hungry wails unnerved the King. The prospect of two crying babies in the castle, he decreed intolerable.

"Why does she refuse to nurse?" the King demanded.

"Because it's a boy. She wanted a girl."

"Tell her it's a girl and to nurse it," the King ordered.

The nursemaids blinked.

"Tell her," said the Chief Steward elaborating the plan, "you made a mistake, and keep the diaper closed. They all look the same at this age."

The shocked women gaped, but followed orders.

To their amazement, the King's Wife, shrugged and took the baby. "I told you it was a girl. I wouldn't have a boy."

The nursemaids objected to calling a boy baby a girl. To keep the hoax working the Chief Steward suggested they simply not refer to the baby with gender words. Call it the baby, but never he or she. He worded his announcement to the provinces the same way--a Child, the King's heir.

The King truly cared not a whit whether a girl or a boy, as long it didn't cry. That disturbing, helpless wail chilled him deep in some primitive memory pocket of his own forgotten infancy. The sound of the baby crying, as it did a great deal, threw him into a frenzy. He burst into the nursery one day and found the crying baby in the cradle while the nursemaids chatted.

"Babies cry," they explained. "There's nothing to be done after they're fed and changed, but let them get over it."

The King could not stand the sound. He discovered, when he picked up the baby to see if something pricked it, the crying ceased. The silence relieved his sensibilities. Thus, whenever he heard the baby cry, he went to the nursery, took it up and carried it about with him. He did not feel particularly affectionate, but when the thing cried and disturbed him, he knew how to fix it and did so. He accepted walking the floor with the baby as another unpleasant imperative. As King, he felt ultimately responsible. It never occurred to him to insist that the nursemaids tend the baby further than basic maintenance. If the baby cried in distress, it must be his fault for bringing the unwanted Child into the world.

The King's Wife, though she nursed, would not leave the baby at her breast long enough to satisfy his hunger or insure proper growth.

"I don't like it gnawing on me," she complained. She seemed aware of the hoax and participated by not calling the baby a girl, but it.

The baby remained thin and worrisome. The Chief Steward suggested extra feedings of goat or cow milk from a wineskin. Cow milk gave the baby stomach cramps which increased the wailing; goat milk caused a violent rash all over his skin. Combined with the wild ranging black hair, which did not disappear fast enough to suit the King, he looked monstrous. The only other alternative was to pump the breasts of the King's Wife for others to feed him her milk.

The girl sobbed and resisted, claiming they milked her like a goat. She accused her husband of using her to get an heir and now he had it, treating her like an animal.

Meanwhile, the sight of the King going about his business with the baby in one arm, for he grew quite adept at carrying it, became a familiar sight in the castle. The nursemaids often delivered the baby to him, after they tended it, before it cried, which suited him best.

The baby developed slowly. The black hair eventually receded, and the eyes opened wider, but the only skills learned early were drinking from a cup and clinging. The Child attached itself to the King's arm or clothing as if an integral part of his person.

Even Tiberius, who laughed at the sight of the ugly little baby, grew used to it. They would be standing at the maps, consulting, or bent over the Chief Steward's supply inventories, when the King would hear the wail. He would wander away mid sentence, and return with the baby. They planned the destruction of Reminnia with a baby clinging on the King's arm.

The Chief Steward occasionally held it, but the Child preferred the King. The Chief Steward decided he could offer more assistance, with education, when the Child got older.

By the time the Child could crawl, and toddle, it toddled after the King, and climbed up his leg into his lap. It slept on the floor, under his table while they plotted and planned. It napped beneath his chair when he sat at court. The court became so accustomed to the King's heir attached to him they soon forgot its presence.

When the King left the castle to accompany Tiberius to inspect the Reminnian wall, no one could comfort the Child. The Chief Steward tried, Lisel tried, the serving women tried. Even the King's Wife, weary of hearing it cry, tried to no avail.

Thus, the first sound greeting the King after his journey, as he entered his castle, was an inconsolable wail. He strode to the nursery and lifted the Child, who quit crying immediately.

"What is this mark on its face?" he inquired of the nursemaids.

At first they did not want to tell him, but at last one confessed. "Your Wife pinched it."

The King felt outraged. When he inspected further, he found more pinch marks. He confronted his Wife, who denied pinching the baby. She claimed the nursemaids did it, because they could not stop it crying, then blamed her. He did not know whom to blame but held the nursemaids responsible.

"Never let her have the baby alone," he ordered, "and, if I find marks on the Child, the nursemaid will be held accountable."

He felt no true affection for this homely Child who did not look like kin to him, but nevertheless a fierce protection. He spent his life trying to make the world safe. The idea a Child would be deliberately hurt in his castle outraged him.

After the youth dispersed from the castle that year, blessed with their adult mantles, the Chief Steward sought Lisel. He found her blending a mix of Lemon Balm, Valerian and Lavender flowers. "Ah, I recognize that." He sighed, deeply inhaling.

"You should," she replied. "You've used quite a bit of it these past weeks."

"Trying times, trying times," he admitted, as he sat down at the table, "but, I shall sleep tonight, without any concoction."

She nodded. "So much work, so many more bodies to tend, and so many decisions. I believe their youthful anxiety permeates the very stones of these walls during the ritual days."

"A tense time," the Chief Steward agreed, "but one matter need no longer concern us. The matter of the sheepherder's nephew is resolved."

Lisel paused, waiting patiently for him to deliver his message. The Chief Steward enjoyed his dramatic moments.

"He will be apprenticed to his uncle."

"Oh, I am so glad!" She reached across the table to touch the old man's hand. "Thank you."

As much as he enjoyed her gratitude, the Chief Steward admitted, "Danny needn't have worried; the young man is lame."

Lisel blinked. The image of the boy bounding and playing the young ram leaped before her eyes. She found nothing lame in her memory.

"Something wrong with his leg, the left one drags from an injury. Tiberius tossed him back with the first culls. He won't be of much use elsewhere, he moves so slowly. Since his uncle wants him, he might as well go there."

"Thank you," Lisel repeated, "for the news, and for the help for Danny."

"I am considering an apprentice myself."

Lisel returned to her work with an ear tuned. She knew him well, and sensed he ruminated deeply about some matter.

The Chief Steward's long fingers traced a groove on the table. "I'm keeping my eye open for a young person I could educate to share my interest in the records. Not this year--next year--I'll know him when I see him."

"Him?" she teased. "You exclude all the girls?"

"A slip of the tongue," he answered quickly. He rose and yawned, hoping to cover his abrupt departure with need of a nap. If he stayed longer he might pour out his entire idea and spoil the surprise.

Claudio would come the next year from the Southeast Province and he intended to take him into the castle family. He would call him an apprentice, or a scholar, and confide only to Lisel his true origins. The King might have another heir, but Lisel would have her son.

Tiberius had observed the King's distraction with domestic problems. Though he never mentioned Child or Wife, while they traveled together inspecting the wall, he noted that the King did not appear as interested in, or insulted by, the insubstantial wall as hoped. Fearing he might change his mind, Tiberius suggested that the King not risk injury.

"A shame to conquer the world and risk losing the King at the last battle." He expected resistance. The King had ridden to every battle and thrilled in the conquest. "Although you've got yourself an heir, I don't think it looks ready for the throne, yet."

The King, walking the floor with the drooling, teething, Child on his shoulder, acquiesced with surprising ease.

"He has no heart for invading Reminnia," the Chief Steward confided later to Lisel. "He gave his word to Tiberius and committed the men and the supplies. He cannot back out so he removes himself."

"Lucky for that pitiful baby," Lisel observed. She marveled how tirelessly, yet without deriving apparent pleasure, he continued to let it cling to him. He did not ask others for assistance. He brought this madness on himself and he coped.

Tiberius selected late Summer to launch against Reminnia. He gauged the weather, the progress on the wall, and counted on the Reminnian Court to take their ships out in the Spring and not return until Fall. The absence of manpower they contained, and at least one, if not both, of the Twin Kings, would assist his conquest. The ships could be met and defeated when they returned. He also gauged his timing to celebrate victory at Grand Parade.

To an uninformed eye, little change appeared. As always, Tiberius kept troops on the move: crossing the plains, shifting commands from one province, one fort, to another. Not only did this keep all his men familiar with the entire country; it prevented any commander from becoming too possessive of one province or fort. As he prepared for his greatest and last offensive, the rotation of troops resulted in a gradual shift of forces south. The Southwest Province fort, closest to where he intended to crack the wall, began to bulge with soldiers. The Southeast Province contained heavy back up, while the northern provinces and castle force lightened.

The Chief Steward calculated supply trains to flow like a cogwheel, funneling water, food, and supplies to the front. With the enemy contained behind their own wall, they calculated less likelihood of counterattack, which pleased the Chief Steward. He needed every shred of positive thought to prepare for a war he deemed unnecessary and imprudent. Nevertheless, he found pleasure exercising his ability to orchestrate on a grand scale. Once the King committed to the action, the Chief Steward ceased argument and worked with unwavering loyalty. He knew, from long experience, what Tiberius needed and where and how to get it there. The synchronization of their efforts restored their companionship during the preparation.

Tiberius wondered why the Chief Steward resisted the war; the old man obviously enjoyed the process.

The Chief Steward racked his brain how to harness this mad dog to peaceful occupations after Reminnia. In the meantime, he made lists based on memory and supposition, of particular books, treasures and items likely to come into their possession during the conquest.

"See, when it's all over, if you can find..."

"When it's all over, you can go to Reminnia and pick through the trash to your hearts content, old man," Tiberius told him.

The Chief Steward did not argue the relative merits of what he called precious and Tiberius labeled trash. Enough that Tiberius displayed a generous mood as he prepared for war. Perhaps his generosity would extend to one young man from the Southeast Province, one Claudio. *Better*, the Chief Steward sighed in his ruminations, *if Claudio could have come of age next year--after Reminnia*. With no battle frontiers ahead, surely the King would not grant Tiberius so many men. It might be easier to get Claudio next year, *but then,* he closed the book, where his finger tracing over the name had almost worn a hole in the page, *who could bear to wait another year?*

War preparations were briefly interrupted in

Spring when the young people who came of age during the past year made their trek to the castle. While Tiberius sorted the young men, taking first choice, the Chief Steward and his Civil Service staff waded through interviewing each young person to determine all the other assignations. Many interviews he delegated to his staff, to make reports, but he always interviewed any considered for castle service. He ticked his personal list to include Claudio and waited with a mix of dread and excitement. After all, the boy might turn up lame, like Danny's nephew, or disappoint him some other way.

Claudio did not turn up lame. The youth who arrived at the Chief Steward's chamber at the appointed hour so shocked the old man with his perfection that, although he kept him an unprecedented amount of time, he could not recall a scrap of their conversation. He remembered the sound of his voice, the intensity of his eyes, and the sensitivity of his manner. The boy's interest in the maps and books overwhelmed the Chief Steward; he had to excuse himself from the interview to regain control. Using the excuse of sharing supper, he returned with food to further prolong the visit. Late in the evening, after he excused Claudio, the old man rested his head on his books and wept. A perfect son who would please Lisel had been restored to them. He sat in the dark recalling how he carried Claudio as a baby into the provinces. How his heart ached--until he wished the worthless thing would break and end its agony. All through Lisel's pregnancy he had campaigned, harder than he campaigned for any other unpopular cause, for Lisel to marry the King. He would have done so, of that the Chief Steward felt certain, but Lisel would not, for some private reason. The reaches of her complicated mind he never fathomed; she simply refused. The King turned his back the night she gave birth. He wanted no details-- except of Lisel's health. Perhaps, thought the Chief Steward, as he compared Claudio with the wispy Child underfoot in the castle, they did the right thing to foster.

Not until he looked at the reports from Tiberius did reality crash like a rock through the window of the old man's dreams. Tiberius selected men in a methodical fashion. He cut out those physically unsuitable and never looked at them again. The best, his first choices, he grouped in another cut and looked at them only as he compared others to them. For the remainder, he measured his allotment against a thorough examination with a scoring system he carried in his head. He sifted men's bodies the way a farmer sifts soil between his fingers. Claudio, Tiberius swept into his first choice group.

The Chief Steward paced his chamber most of the day, after receiving that report. Naturally, he should have predicted it. Though not focused on Claudio's physical capabilities, any fool with eyes could see his perfection. For one in the middle group, over whom Tiberius weighed and considered, the

Chief Steward might have negotiated. Over one of his precious first choices, never. Pleading would only make the brute clamp his fist tighter.

Explaining to Tiberius, in confidence, that Claudio was Lisel's first born son and they must restore him to her, seemed logical in the middle of the night. He would wake in the wee hours to find himself mid-sentence composing his case. By light of day he recognized the idea as a figment of fantasy. If Tiberius knew, he would want the King's son for himself.

The Chief Steward decided to steal Claudio from Tiberius. He began to watch for a way--like slipping through the edge of a dark forest avoiding the enemy. He never liked that sort of risk, but had done so many times and survived. Now he must slip through the forest of prime young men Tiberius claimed, and snatch one for himself--not for himself--for Lisel.

Tiberius did not keep written records to refer to at the ceremony. He knew how many men he chose from each province and nicked them off on the edge of the table with his dagger. Sometimes he dozed through long lines of women and men he did not want. Of his own, he recognized most, but on those over which he debated, he often looked to the Chief Steward with the record book for a cue. This year, Tiberius' attention focused on the assault soon to be waged on Reminnia. Beyond taking his last cut of officers, he had little use for the ceremonies. The Chief Steward saw these as points to dart and hide

123

while making his raid.

On the morning of the ceremony he planned to give the doorkeeper instructions to keep the line moving faster than usual. The Southeast Province, with Claudio, came after the Northeast. Tiberius' interest would be dulled. The final mark in the book also fell to the Chief Steward's advantage. He knew he could not take one, without giving one; Tiberius would count his pups like a wild bitch. If he came out short, he would be rabid. One exchange early in the C's would not--must not--be noticed. The Chief Steward noted that young man exactly before Claudio on the list, Chad, was one over whom Tiberius debated. He put him in, took him out, put him back, so many times the page should be recopied. Instead, with a few deft strokes, the Chief Steward extended the smudge to remove Claudio as it restored Chad.

At the banquet, the night before the ceremony, Lisel noticed the ebullient spirits of the Chief Steward. "You look exceptionally well," she commented as they sat side by side at the table.

"An exceptionally fine group of youth this year. I am quite inspired by them," he replied. Lisel glanced over the hall and agreed they looked bright and eager. "One in particular pleases me," the Chief Steward could not resist adding. "I found an apprentice, a scholar."

"Still the Tutor at heart," she commented with a

smile. "A lucky one to be chosen by you."

"You will see, you will see," he said, then bit his tongue. He must not confide his secret in the noisy banquet hall. Later, tomorrow, he would tell her-- restore to her a magnificent son. At the opposite end of the head table, Tiberius flirted with the King's Wife. The Chief Steward chuckled, imagining sneaking up, like a thief, on Tiberius. The idea enormously amused him.

The next morning, the King and Tiberius appreciated how the Chief Steward whipped the line along at a good clip. Usually they complained that he dragged it out to enjoy the ritual. The Chief Steward told the door attendants to crank even faster as they began the Southeast Province line. His own heart also began to beat faster as he opened the Southeast book. First came the women. Tiberius dozed--preferable to his bored agitation, scraping his bench on the stone floor.

Then came the men. Tiberius woke and sat straight at his table. Cold perspiration flowed under the Chief Steward's robes. The three began their visual dance. As the clerk announced the name, Tiberius and the Chief Steward exchanged glances, then one signaled the King with flick of the hand.

As perfectly, as if planned, Tiberius looked for a cue to recollect his final decision on Chad. The Chief Steward nodded to Tiberius; Chad disappeared into the ranks with the officers. Half the deed had been accomplished--but no time to pause, not even to wipe away perspiration. Claudio, next in line, advanced. With only a cursory glance that did not connect with Tiberius, the Chief Steward signaled the King to direct this one to Castle Service.

Tiberius needed no prompt for Claudio. He signaled the King to send him for an officer.

The King waited for one to withdraw. Never had there been a discrepancy at this moment. No matter how they wrangled beforehand, they arrived at the ritual in agreement, with the bookkeeping in impeccable order. Now they stood, resolved to disagree.

Tiberius kicked over his bench. "MINE!"

The Chief Steward clutched the book, which would prove him correct. The King never looked at the book, not even when Tiberius accused the Chief Steward of changing it. He dismissed Claudio to the guard; the moment was lost. The next young man thrust himself upon them.

By the end of the day, which continued at a pace much too fast to suit the devastated Chief Steward, the King appeared to have forgotten the incident. Tiberius considered it a joke, since he triumphed and gained an extra man. To Lisel, who heard about the fracas from the shocked clerk, the Chief Steward said only, "Tiberius wanted him, and the King favors him." The only good thought to rest his weary head that night--he had not told her about her son, then lost him to Tiberius for this senseless war.

The banquet before Tiberius' departure for Reminnia, was small. Most of his troops waited impatiently in the southern provinces and on the low plains. Nevertheless, the absence of women and the rattle of war marked the occasion as no ordinary dinner party. The Chief Steward excused himself early, after the formalities. The King lingered late, torn by his decision not to go to battle. He almost changed his mind.

Tiberius discouraged him. "Don't risk. What good to conquer the world and lose the King in some stupid accident?"

Somewhere in the castle the Child cried. Although no one else heard it in the drunken male din, the King heard the wail. He heard both a child in need and an heir, awaiting his death. He accepted Tiberius' advice. He would not go.

Tiberius, and his officers, rode out at dawn. The King walked down to the gate but unable to tolerate the sight of them riding to war without him, turned his back the moment Jurgius ordered the gate closed.

The Chief Steward, watching from the wall, lingered. His eyes did not deceive him! The Junior Officer attending Jurgius was Claudio! He had not seen him since the day he lost him among the throng herded out to be trained in the low plains. He grieved him lost forever, but there stood Claudio--tall, hard and expressionless now, like other officers, but no mistaking him. Reminnia might be conquered, untold numbers of men crushed against that wall, but Claudio would not be among them. A rush of joy flooded the Chief Steward. He felt so light headed another bright idea hatched. Lisel had more children yet to come of age. He would check his record books that very morning, before his attention must focus on war reports and supply requests. Before any bad news arrived from Reminnia to dim his hope for the future, he would find her next child--a girl--if he recalled correctly, which he always did. Tiberius could not take a girl from him!

Lisel, watching from a high window, did not flatter herself to think she manipulated Tiberius' interest south instead of north. She felt the strong shadow of the Mountain behind her and leaned upon its presence. One woman could not protect it, and neither could one man conquer it.

Once she felt driven to go and explore. Now she heard the Mountain King say, "I have not such a complex Kingdom, and frankly, very little work beyond the care of my flocks."

The Mountain, she decided, as the rising sun changed its color, did not need her as much as she needed it. She would be wise to see the outcome of the venture against Reminnia before leaving this Court.

The Chief Steward looked up and waved to her. She raised her hand to return his greeting. Many times she stood next to him, watching Tiberius and the King ride out, with mixed dread and hope. Now they stood apart. For the first time Lisel hoped for crushing defeat. She drew her shawl tightly with fists clenched.

Through the hot summer the King passed tedious, yet anxious, afternoons with Lisel and the Chief Steward. Though little comfort to each other, the men gravitated to a particular shady courtyard each afternoon where they often found Lisel.

At first, runners arrived daily with news regarding the progress of troops toward Reminnia. Abruptly, after report of the first break in the wall, the reports ceased.

"I should be with him," the King fretted. "He knows I can't tolerate lack news. So if news does not come, it means it can't...because..."

"No news is not bad news," the Chief Steward tried to soothe him, but his words rang hollow.

"No news is not good news," the King snapped.

"No news," Lisel said, "is simply no news."

"Now you know what it's like." The Chief Steward fanned himself, worn out from pacing. "Waiting and waiting...worrying about both of you. How many times, Lisel?"

Lisel shrugged. She had lost count and interest in the number of times she and the Chief Steward waited to see if the King and Tiberius would return, and if so, with what wounds to be dressed.

"This time," the Chief Steward continued, calculating the worst case scenario, "it would not be a disaster if he did not press all the way to conquest."

"His life is my concern, not conquest," snapped the King. "I should be with him. We have saved each other's lives many times. What good am I here?"

A sigh from the Child napping under his chair answered him.

Thus many long hot afternoons frittered away in contemplations which took them far ranging directions. The King fretted for the safety of Tiberius. The Chief Steward considered the political implications of failure to achieve conquest. Lisel contemplated a world without Tiberius.

Jurgius took it upon himself to report every afternoon even when no runner arrived with news. Unwittingly he became associated with the continual report of no news which the King, in spite of the Chief Steward's counsel, viewed as bad news. As Castle Fort Commander, Jurgius had little do and felt demeaned to be left behind with only a small group of officers, too young or too old, for battle. Once he believed Tiberius groomed him to inherit his command. As time passed, he saw little evidence the command would come soon enough to be worth his patience. He did not consider Tiberius might be killed in battle; he worried that others would return with tales and trophies. He would play no part in this campaign which obsessed Tiberius for years. Some new hero would eclipse him. His irritation lashed out at all who crossed his shadow.

Jurgius reported to the King every afternoon,

wheedling for orders to take a search party south. One runner could be delayed, or injured, even killed, but no runners for as many days as now passed appeared ominous. At least, Jurgius liked to make it sound ominous, hoping for importance in the King's eye. The matter, and the officer bringing it to his attention, did increase in importance--like a festering splinter-- in the King's eye.

Privately the King considered sending a search party south, but not Jurgius. Since the fiasco of the Mountain King's death, and the lost horse episode, the King scorned his judgement. If Jurgius influenced him any direction, it was to disregard his agitation and wait another day.

One day, near sundown, a great commotion commenced at the castle gate. The King rushed out to look over the wall. From above he saw Jurgius manhandling a runner, black with the dust of the road. The runner had fallen from his horse in the gateway. The exhausted man could not defend himself from Jurgius' blows, and the young officers at the gate dared not interfere with their commander.

The runner's worst offense, it appeared, was refusal to give the message to Jurgius. "For the King, for the King," he gasped.

"I take messages to the King. Speak to me."

"To the King," the runner insisted.

"Bring him to me," ordered the King, from above on the wall.

Jurgius hauled the man up and thrust him at two junior officers. "Take him to the King."

As a prisoner, rather than the long awaited messenger, they dragged the runner into the courtyard before the King, the Chief Steward and Lisel.

Stripped to a loincloth for a hard ride in the heat of summer, the runner fell down, trembling, hands over his head, moaning as if expecting another blow.

"The message?" Jurgius demanded, nudging him with his boot.

"To the King," said the runner.

"I am here." The King knelt to hear him. "Tell me."

The others pressed close to hear him whisper. "From Tiberius to the King." He paused to snatch another breath. "We are victorious at Reminnia."

Expecting the worst, all staggered back at the unexpected good news. Yet the runner, as if he delivered bad news, sobbed in his hands.

"What's the matter with him?" growled Jurgius. "He brings news of victory as if we are defeated."

"He is ill," Lisel pronounced, pushing through the group of men with a dipper of water. "Only a sip," she warned as she lifted his head.

"Is there more to the message?" asked the Chief Steward.

The runner shook his head. "From Tiberius to the King. We are victorious at Reminnia." Still he trembled, though Lisel's dipper of water and soft hand somewhat restored his wits.

"You know something that distresses you--something more terrible than the joy of victory?" the King pressed.

The runner groaned; his body rocked with agony.

"What?" demanded the Chief Steward. "What?"

"Tiberius?" The King seized the runner, raising him to look in his face. "Is Tiberius alive?"

"I left him alive, but wounded so--I don't know how he sits his horse. Grey as death...yet alive."

"Wounded? Where?" The King could scarcely restrain himself from shaking the man who swooned and fell limp in his hands.

"Chest," the runner blurted, and sobbed anew.

"But he sent no message about his wound?" the King gently shook him to open his eyes. The only response was a negative dangling of the head.

"Then he has no business to report it," Jurgius asserted. "A runner reports what he is told, not what he observes on his own."

"Quiet." The King's arm shot out so quickly that Jurgius stepped back to avoid a blow. "What else did you see to trouble you so?"

The runner leaned on Lisel. "Such destruction...I have never seen...old men...women and children..."

"Killed?" asked the Chief Steward.

"And killing..." The runner now revived enough to be embarrassed by his discomfiture and spoke in a rush to defend himself. "I am not new to war. I have seen bloodshed, but nothing like this."

"Lock him up," Jurgius ordered. "If word of Tiberius wounded and this fool's hysteria get loose..."

"Already a crowd gathers," the Chief Steward observed, closing the door.

"They fear the worst because of this blubbering runner," Jurgius said.

"Announce the victory as Tiberius sent the word," the King decided. "Say no more."

"And put this fool under lock until Tiberius arrives," Jurgius said. "We'll see how he judges a runner who distorts his victory message with slobbering."

"He will come with me," Lisel said. "The man suffers from sun stroke."

Jurgius gave way. Lisel remained a fortress he could not storm.

The King forgot the runner; only the injury to Tiberius mattered. "I should have been with him."

"I'll go meet him on the road," Jurgius decided.

"You'll go nowhere," the King ordered. "If he wanted you, he'd send for you." In the same breath he quelled his own impulse to dash to Tiberius' side.

"He has aid by now," the Chief Steward reminded him. "Supply wagons roll every day."

"The voice of reason, as always, old man." The King fondly put an arm around the Chief Steward. "We will announce victory, together."

While Lisel co-opted the officers to carry the runner, now passed into fever and chills, to her quarters, the King and Chief Steward went forward to address the gathering crowd.

Jurgius, left useless again, snarled at the Child under the King's chair. "Ugly brat."

The King's Wife came flying down the corridor and collided with the King and Chief Steward as they returned from making the announcement. "We won! I just heard the news!"

"Yes. So has everyone," said the King. His disposition did not appear improved by good news. His Wife stopped so short in her enthusiastic rush, it almost appeared as if he struck her. "You now rule the whole world!" she said, changing to a coy flirtatious mode. "May I be first to congratulate you?"

"No, you may not," retorted the King. "Until Tiberius returns we have nothing to celebrate." He brushed past her.

Runners began to arrive again in daily sequence. They reported that the victory held and spoils were being taken. Tiberius expected to return soon, but no word came about his injury. Jurgius dismissed the first runner as addled by the sun, but the King did not discount the extraneous report. He heard more detailed and sobering reports of a surprisingly barbarous response from the supposedly genteel Reminnians. Perhaps they did not have true victory. They might be undefeated, without being victorious. He recognized the difference, but as long as daily reports arrived from Tiberius, he knew him to be alive. Victory mattered less in the reports than the life of the sender.

Under Lisel's care, the heat stroked runner regained his health, though he would never have the stamina to run again in battle.

"We will have no more battles," the Chief Steward consoled the anguished man. "We will work for resettlement where runners travel at a more civilized pace."

On the day the Commander in Chief rode through the castle gates with a retinue of battle torn officers, the King ran down to greet him. Tiberius' face, jaw set in a permanent grimace against pain, indeed looked gray as death. His chest, with one arm bound against it, was wrapped in a blood soaked bandage. As he helped him dismount, the full weight of the brute fell against the King nearly taking them both to the ground.

"Hold me," Tiberius grunted, "up!" He would not be seen wounded and weak at the moment he returned victorious over Reminnia.

The King supported Tiberius, half dragging him up the castle steps where the Chief Steward rushed to meet them. The people saw the invincible three united again, victorious as always. They dismissed rumors of a serious wound to Tiberius.

Lisel did not hurry to see Tiberius' wound. That she took her time further convinced people his wound could not be serious.

"What happened?" The King almost wept as Tiberius slumped to the floor the moment they stepped out of the public eye.

"Chest wound." Tiberius flinched. "Don't touch it. Still breaks and bleeds."

"And stinks," the Chief Steward noted. "How long ago?"

"Awhile. Didn't kill me then--won't now."

"Rot can kill you," said the Chief Steward. "Send for Lisel."

"I already sent for her," said the King, but so anxious was he to care for his wounded friend, he began to undo his boots and belts himself. "Get water," he ordered the Chief Steward. "I'll bathe him myself."

When Lisel arrived, she found the King stripped to work, bathing Tiberius' limbs, lamenting each nick and bruise on the old dog. Even the Chief Steward had pushed up his sleeves and dirtied his hands to sponge Tiberius' feet, though neither dared touch the rag that bound Tiberius' arm to his chest. She watched for a moment in the doorway--how those three loved each other.

Tiberius rolled his head toward her and grimaced. "Lisel. You--only you--look at my chest."

Lisel had dressed his wounds many times, though none so deep as this, and never had she been disappointed to see him return alive. She didn't realize until he flashed his ornery grin, how strongly she counted on him being returned dead. She could have prepared his body for burial, concentrating on the years she respected his loyalty to the King, recalling times he had protected her, and remembering his moments of kindness to the old man. Alive, she hated him. Nevertheless she began unwinding the grimy bandage, stiff with blood. The King and Chief Steward stepped back.

"Leave me alone with him," she asked.

"You, old man." Tiberius yanked the Chief Steward by the arm. "Do this." He hauled him down to whisper in his ear.

The Chief Steward listened and blinked-- shocked, though hard to tell whether by the request, or the odor. Agreement appeared the only response that would release his arm.

"Now!" Tiberius ordered and winced in pain.

The Chief Steward glanced at Lisel and the King, then rushed to do Tiberius' errand.

"You should go, too," Lisel urged the King. "This is an ugly wound; don't watch."

"I cannot bear to leave him." The King insisted on holding Tiberius' head in his lap.

The wound began to bleed. Tiberius groaned and closed his eyes. Safe out of sight of any but his trusted intimates, he submitted to his pain and to Lisel's ministrations.

The thought occurred to Lisel, *let him bleed to death*. Without the King cradling his head, looking anxiously from his face to hers, she might have watched his lifeblood run out. Who would know she had not done all she could for him?

Lisel did not like finding such cruel notions in her head, though any other course felt like weakness. She excused her weakness, because of the watchful eye of the King, and cleansed the wound. Tiberius passed into the oblivion he had needed for days as she cleaned the rotting flesh.

"Why does he bleed, still?" begged the King.

"Not a large wound," Lisel observed, "but deep."

Once cleaned, she should dress it with healing herbs. She could dress it with poisonous herbs, if she had any. She knew them well enough, to avoid them. Murder refused again to come to her hands, though never had she wanted a man dead more than this one. Even for invaders, in old times, she felt some grief as they fell--seeing them as foolish men, and in their death, surprised, disappointed and hurt.

Unfair, unfair! She choked back her tears. *He went to battle, got a deadly wound, yet did not die. Why does he live and good men, who harm no one, die*?

"Will he live?" the King asked anxiously.

Lisel shrugged, unable to answer. She wrapped the wound well, the only way she knew, and excused herself. Other wounded officers continued to arrive needing attention.

The King intended to sit with Tiberius all night but the Chief Steward returned, quite distressed. He insisted that the King come with him to the cellar where the spoils of war were being unloaded.

"I care nothing about the spoils, only his life," the King said. "Do as you please with them."

"You must decide about this yourself," the Chief Steward begged. "You must."

Tiberius slept. Reluctantly, the King followed the Chief Steward to the cellar.

Later that night, the harried Chief Steward met Lisel in the passage returning from the barracks where she had overseen the care of a number of wounded men. He apologized for asking her to see one more patient but she would gladly postpone checking on Tiberius.

"How is Tiberius?" he asked as they walked.

"The wound is deep, from a dagger, but not wide. If whoever drove it so deep would have turned it, that would have finished him on the spot." She did not care if the Chief Steward heard regret in her voice.

"A woman wounded him. She might not have known to twist a dagger, or perhaps lost her grip."

"A woman?" Lisel caught up a step to match the Chief Steward's pace.

"A woman, that much he told me."

She recalled the first runner telling how the women, ferocious though unskilled, engaged in the combat. Still, the idea shocked her.

The Chief Steward unlocked the door to the cellars and began the downward spiral to storerooms where the spoils of war were delivered. Late at night now, the work had ceased; piles of goods stood heaped in the passages and open areas. "So much ruined," he waved a hand. "Ruined by rough handling. No need to drag it here. If they had left it alone, I could have gone there."

"The person you want me to tend is down here?" Lisel questioned, following him through the corridors of the storage cellars.

"I am afraid to move her," he said.

"Her?" Lisel caught her shawl more tightly on her shoulder.

In a dark, but cool, quiet area of the cellar, the Chief Steward held the lamp to illuminate the body of a woman, lying face down on the stone floor. "She's not moved since I last checked her. She may be dead."

Lisel bent quickly and rolled the woman over, to feel her pulse. The eyelids fluttered but the eyes did not focus. Olive skin, long dark tangled hair, slightly built, once quite beautiful, though now looking as battle ragged as any of the men, Lisel observed. "Who is she?"

"The Reminnian woman who stabbed him," the Chief Steward said. "He wants her kept alive."

Lisel, kneeling by the unconscious woman, stared in disbelief. "Tiberius took a prisoner?"

The Chief Steward wagged his head. "I do not know the full story," he said, though he did not tell her all he did know. He dared not confess to Lisel that the woman whose hand she held was the conquered

Queen of Reminnia. The idea frightened him so he scarcely admitted it to himself.

"Does the King know?"

The Chief Steward nodded, looking miserable. "He turned his back."

"And so do I!" Lisel rose and drew back her skirt.

"Lisel? Please, help her--a woman--even if Reminnian. How can you refuse?"

"Precisely because she is a woman," Lisel scolded him. "What remains in life for a woman taken prisoner by Tiberius?"

"I don't know, I don't know," mourned the Chief Steward. "I can't believe he did this, but he did, and the King will deny him nothing now. He turned his back. He said 'Spoils of War.' We can't let her suffer."

"She's not suffering," Lisel replied. "She's unconscious. If we don't tend her she will die before HE regains the strength to come for her."

"Lisel..."

"No! And, if you know what's best in the long view, you will not prolong her life, either."

Outraged, Lisel took the lamp from his hand and headed for the stairs. The Chief Steward, rather than be left in the dark with the woman on the floor, stumbled after her. At the top of the stairs, they turned opposite directions.

"I have patients to tend," she dismissed him.

After the Chief Steward departed, Lisel leaned against the wall, heart pounding, horrified by what she had seen below. Confusion overwhelmed her; in her heart she longed to dash back down the stairs to the unconscious woman, hide her and tend her. Her realistic self warned her that the Reminnian woman would be better dead than revived as Tiberius' property--spoils! The King would give her no quarter, not even as woman, after threatening Tiberius' life. He would turn his back and let Tiberius mete out whatever punishment he chose when he recovered.

Tiberius, the brute, nevertheless her patient, should be checked. Reluctant feet carried her to his door. She expected to find the King holding his hand, but Tiberius lay alone on his cot.

She listened to his labored breath.

He sensed a presence at his doorway. "Water."

She did not rush to fill the cup. Pausing in the doorway, she considered how she decided to let the Reminnian woman die.

"Water."

If she could let the woman die, could she let Tiberius die? She found more than enough justification to do so in his atrocities, starting with the Mountain King, including that woman below and a myriad other actions she did not have to know to believe he had done.

"Water."

Lisel turned resolutely from his door. She met the King hurrying down the passage and caught his arm. "The Chief Steward told you about the woman Tiberius brought from Reminnia?"

"He told you, too?" His eyes refused to meet hers.

"He asked me to tend her. She is near death."

"Yes, I could see."

So, he has not only been told, but seen the condition of that woman, she realized.

"Could you help her?"

"No. She will most likely die before morning."

The King nodded. "Just as well, but don't tell Tiberius. He wants her to live."

Lisel found no words to express her rage.

"How is he? I left him to tend the Child and a number of other things delayed me."

Gently, but firmly, she placed her hand on his arm. "Tiberius is asleep. Don't disturb him."

She felt his hand cover hers, torn between running to Tiberius and staying with her in this moment of rarely offered physical affection.
"I just checked him. Come, let's share a cup of wine-- a long disturbing day for both of us."

"If he's asleep," the King said slowly, sorting his thoughts as he spoke. "I presume I need you more than he needs me. I surely won't sleep."

"Nor I," Lisel agreed. "Come with me." She led him to his private chamber. She opened the window to the starry sky and view of the mountains beyond. They were snow capped even in summer, and visible in the moonlight.

He poured wine and poured out his heart, his life, his woe, and his fear for Tiberius' health. The well being of those he loved mattered most to the King. If one were lost, ruling the world would be worthless. He said he supposed she also felt the threat to their circle. He believed shared concern for Tiberius brought her affection back to him that worrisome night.

Lisel listened and soothed him. She drew him out, urging him to talk more, remember more, while she counted the hours until dawn. She would even make love him to him, if necessary, to prevent him from going to Tiberius.

While the King and Lisel shared repose and wine in the window under the stars, the King's Wife roamed the castle. Hustled aside during the excitement, she had caught no more than a glimpse of Tiberius as they helped him to his chamber. Now, in the silence of the night, she tiptoed past his door. Finding no one, especially not her husband or Lisel, in attendance, she stepped inside to stare at the huge, scarred body stretched on the cot.

His breath came ragged, as if it must circumvent the wound in his chest. His eyes were closed; maybe he slept. She moved closer to see him better in the moonlight. From that vantagepoint, she studied his body with frank interest. He had always excited her, making her shiver with delicious dread, but rarely did she get so close to him. She had never seen him exposed, as he lay that night, after throwing off the cover, irritated by anything touching his fevered body.

She remembered how hot he felt when he touched her hand in greeting, or brushed against her in a crowd. She wondered if he would wake if she touched him. On the night he came to her chamber, before her marriage to the King, she felt frightened at how her pulse raged out of control. Now she enjoyed the brew of fear and pleasure tingling at the core of her body. She longed to put a finger to his arm, or his leg--see if he felt hot. Fearing that Lisel would arrive to stop her, if she hesitated longer, she quickly touched his foot. Hot! Horribly hot!

He flinched, as if a fly stung him.

She wanted to touch him again, and feel his flesh, hot and terrible, under her fingers. While she hesitated, his rough hand seized her by the wrist, pulling her so she almost fell on his wounded chest.

"Water!"

"Let go so I can pour your water," she whispered. She still feared some official keeper would rush in to steal him from her.

He released her arm but rolled an eye to watch the cup. Hard to tell if he focused enough to recognize her, but he gripped her hand as she held the cup to his lips. After only a few drops he sputtered, pushing it aside. "Fever," he muttered.

No one arrived to shoo her away from the man she found most exciting in the entire kingdom.

"Shall I put a cool rag on your head?"

He rumbled but didn't answer.

She wrung out the towel left by the basin, and wiped his face. He clamped his hand around her wrist again to prevent her from leaving him.

"Let go and I'll bathe you."

He moaned some sort of assent.

With great excitement, she dipped the towel again and began to bathe his body. The towel turned hot the instant it touched his body. In the dim light she imagined steam rising from his limbs. When she finished, he seemed relaxed. She sat by him, feasting her eyes on his delicious body--totally in her care.

"Water."

She gave him water. Then she refilled the basin and bathed him again. Why not? He liked it and she liked touching him.

The King and Lisel found her the next morning, asleep by Tiberius' side. His hand was clamped around her wrist. The damp cloth dangled from her hand. The water pitcher stood empty. Tiberius slept with a less ragged breath than last night.

"Look," marveled the King. "I didn't know she had a drop of kindness in her."

Lisel turned away from the sight of the King gently waking his Wife and congratulating her for her kindness. Heading for her chamber, she scarcely watched which way she went and bumped into the Chief Steward.

"How is Tiberius?" he asked.

"Better than I expected."

She did not ask and he did not dare tell her that he had been early to the cellar. Finding the Queen of Reminnia still alive, he could no longer tolerate the agony. He sent two serving women, sworn to secrecy, downstairs to tend her.

Lisel tried to take comfort that the destruction happened in Reminnia, not on the Mountain with Tiberius hunting for horses, but found no contentment in her thoughts. She feared that the part of her, which might have risen to meet the expectations of the Mountain King, had been destroyed with him. Only in his eyes was she a Queen. With those eyes closed in death, she found it difficult to sustain the image of herself as Queen of the Mountain.

"Perhaps, after all, I am only a common woman who had some uncommon experiences."

In the meantime people needed her care. She had herbs to cultivate, harvest and prepare. A new crop of lambs dotted the hills beyond the castle. She went about her daily tasks with diligence, yet with heaviness of heart.

When the King's glance fell on Lisel he saw her color fading, her hair turning gray. She might be dying, as he so recently feared for Tiberius, but he could do nothing for her. He spoke to the Chief Steward, who had been her first love. If anyone could restore her spirit, he might be the one.

"I too have observed her failing," the Chief

Steward agreed. "I am looking for a young woman to attend her."

"Attend her? You think she is that ill?"

"It would have been better if the Mountain King had lived long enough for her to grow weary of him," said the Chief Steward, "as it is..."

The King did not want to recall the Mountain King. "Surely, among so many women here, one could help her?"

"Lisel has been healer and confidant to all of them. She would never submit to their care. No, I must find a new young woman. I will look this Spring when they come from the provinces."

He had long since marked the place in his book, but did not tell the King, or Lisel, that he planned to restore one of her daughters to her. After the dismal failure with Claudio, he did not trust even his best-laid plans.

Some nights Lisel dreamed of the olive skinned woman with the dark tangled hair and the fluttering eyelids. In her dreams, she gathered the broken woman into her arms and ran with her to the Mountain.

"We both tried, though neither of us killed him." Consoling and forgiving, making peace for all the wrongs between them, Lisel would wrap the unconscious woman in her soft white shawl like a infant. The body felt light in her arms. In dreams, they flew up and over the boulders in the road to the safety of the Mountain.

After the visitation of this recurrent dream, Lisel woke strangely comforted. Her limbs, which usually seemed heavy, felt new strength. Deep in the innermost chamber of her heart a small lamp still illuminated her vision. *One day*, she privately trusted, *the way up the Mountain will open--as easy as flying there in dreams.*

THE END